Resurrecting

Mingus

A Novel

Jenoyne Adams

The Free Press

New York London Toronto Sydney Singapore

*f*P

THE FREE PRESS
A Division of Simon & Schuster, Inc.
1230 Avenue of the Americas
New York, NY 10020

THE FREE PRESS and colophon are registered trademarks of
Simon & Schuster, Inc.
Book design by Susan Hood
Manufactured in the United States of America
10 9 8 7 6 5 4 3 2 1

Library of Congress Cataloging-in-Publication Data
Adams, Jenoyne.
   Resurrecting Mingus : a novel / Jenoyne Adams.
      p.   cm.
1. Racially mixed people—Fiction.   2. Young women—Fiction.
   I. Title.
PS3551.D3745 R47 2001
813'.6—dc21
                                                           00-052077
ISBN 0-684-87352-4

This book is dedicated to the five pillars in my life: my father, Virgil; my mother, Bertha; my sister, Jolena; my friend Edgar L. Brown; and my beautiful husband, Michael Datcher.

Resurrecting Mingus

For none of us liveth to himself,
and no man dieth to himself.

Romans 14:7

Chapter 1

June 3

He left her for a black woman. Eva called first thing Saturday morning to make sure I heard it from her first. Punk Ass Nigga.

She lay on the couch, butt cheeks wedged between cracked leather cushions, knees pressed into her swollen breasts. It was this position she hated most—being twisted into a pretzel by 4:00 A.M. sweats and contractions riding each other piggyback across her abdomen.

With the windows shut, the room held the musty scent of unstirred air. The smell nauseated her. Mingus swallowed the acid in the back of her throat and made her way down the unlit hall to the bathroom. A vanilla candle rolled in coffee beans sat next to her perfume tray. She grazed her fingers across the cold porcelain counter, locating a book of matches. The candle flame illuminated her flat stomach and cast dancing shadows across the knee imprints on her breasts. She leaned in toward the mirror. Fuzzy ringlets of almost black hair tickled her lips. With both hands, she parted the hair like a curtain down the middle of her face, making a clearing for her eyes. She could feel them coming on again. Contractions with sharp bony fingers burrowed into the walls of her pelvis. The blood would start to flow soon.

Mingus kicked the cotton underwear from around her ankles and lowered herself into the tub. Water gushed over her unpainted toes. Massaging currents gathered between her thighs. The water was soothing, but it was no consolation for seventeen years' worth of periods. She was empty again.

The roundness of her breasts buoyed in the water. Mingus rested her head against the green tiled wall and clasped her hands over her naval. Her stomach was warm like freshly cooling muffins. Pressing her fingers into her belly, she felt energy stir below the surface. She hoped it wouldn't come this time. Even though Keith was the wrong one. Even though they used protection. Even though they broke up almost a month ago, when he decided that moving back to New York, *without her,* was best for his career. She splashed her face. I'm not gonna cry, I'm not gonna cry, she repeated in a quiet breath.

A heavy procession of blood moved down her uterus. She felt it coming. Mingus crossed her legs; her vaginal lips pulsed from the tightness of her hold. Blood pooled at the entrance of her womb. She looked down. A thin stream of crimson ribboned under her thighs. She watched as it dissolved slowly in the slight sway of water. Her vision blurred from the tears filling her eyes, but not one fell. She uncrossed her legs. The color of ripe beets flooded the water. Within moments, she sat in a uniform shade of pink. Empty.

The water was lukewarm when the phone rang. Mingus threw her bathing sponge past the bathroom door into the hallway. Suds splattered the wall, leaving drip lines on the flat latex paint. *Ring.* There was no one she wanted to talk to. No one who could save her from splintering. She groped the sides of the tub and vertebrae by vertebrae stood up. Pale sudsy water ran down her legs. She stepped onto the lime green floor mat and pulled a towel from the brass bar. The towel was rough against her skin. She rubbed it over her breast, onto her stomach, between her legs. She rubbed hardest between her legs.

Mingus walked past the couch to her desk with the blood-stained towel in her hand. She sat, her nude spine curving like a newly wilted flower toward the phone. What if it was Keith, she thought. It made sense with the hour time difference. Maybe he missed her. Maybe he realized he'd made a mistake.

The phone rang again.

"Hello."

"You cryin'?"

Mingus didn't answer. She bunched the towel to her mouth and tried to steady the dampness in her voice.

"Sound like you busy or somethin'. You got a nigga over there?"

Her breath was hot and moist at the same time. Heat radiated through the towel into her cupped fingers.

"You may as well tell it, dick is a good thing. You ain't got to be shame."

"It's none of your business, Eva."

"Ooooh, you nasty this morning. He musta stood you up, huh?"

Mingus ripped a sheet of paper from the spiral notebook in front of her and began to pick off the broken edges. She didn't know why her relationships kept blowing up like this. She'd thought she'd done things right this time. Made him wait a few months before having sex. Didn't fuss about his schedule. Only called a couple times a week. This one was supposed to be different.

"And you playing the silent treatment," Eva said, rattling her attitude like a fast-flying epithet. "I didn't have to call you. Shoulda left your ass in the dark, that's what I shoulda did—M'Dea wasn't going to tell you nothin' no way."

It never amazed Mingus how easily Eva switched from kind to cold; it was Eva's mention of their mother that made her nervous.

"What happened?"

"You sure you wanna know?"

"Don't play with me Eva, all right. Not today."

Eva smacked her lips and let out a heavy sigh. "You know how Carl's been trippin' and stuff right?"

"Yeah," Mingus said, not knowing what Eva was talking about.

"Well, looks like he *does* have another woman."

Mingus felt the muscles tense in her forehead. "I don't know why you keep making stuff up, Eva. He's your father. Don't you get tired of this?"

"He's *your* father. And you're a damn fool if you can't see what's going on. The man don't come home for days at a time. What you think he's doin'?" Eva smacked then paused for dramatic effect. "Only difference between then and now is that this time we got proof. M'Dea found his letters in the tool shed."

There was surety in Eva's voice. Mingus tore another sheet of paper from the notebook and began to doodle inadvertently.

"She's sure it's another woman?"

"Didn't you take logic or something in law school? What else could it be, they've been married thirty-five years. You know what they say, new puss—"

"I gotta go."

"Whatever, but if you planning to call M'Dea, which you are, you may as well hang it up. She ain't answering the phone."

Click. Mingus sat at the desk with the unhooked receiver pulsing a dial tone between her thighs. Her mind was full. A salad spinner gone mad with no lid. She reminded herself to focus on what she could control. Stop sleeping on the couch, Mingus, she thought. She grabbed the pillow from the couch and headed into the bedroom. On tiptoe, she outstretched her arms and placed the plain white pillow above the stacked sheets in the utility cabinet. One by one she pulled the perfectly folded sheets onto the floor. Comforters to the floor. Pillowcases to the floor. They needed to be restacked. All of them. Refolded and restacked. The coffee cup.

Mingus grabbed a pillowcase from the pile at her feet and walked over to the bed. An empty coffee cup sat on the nightstand. Kenyan roast dripped hardened chocolate lines down the curves of the cup, leaving a circle on the blond oak. She covered her index finger in a corner of the pillowcase and began to wipe the stain. The softness of the fabric made it smooth. Smooth so that its hardness rounded but didn't disappear. She could have scraped it away, let the sugary brownness collect under her nails, but it wouldn't have changed anything. She was alone again. And after thirty-five years, M'Dea's bed was now empty.

The house was the color of mustard seed, tucked behind tufts of pine and sweet gum trees on County Road 320. Beyond the trees, visible from the kitchen window, was a small lake stocked with catfish and Gasper Goo. The tires kicked up dust as Mingus curved around the gravel driveway past the lake. The house looked the same. She hadn't expected it to. Pink and fuchsia zinnias lined the flagstone walk. Spanish-style brick laced in ivy arched the double door entrance.

With brass knocker in hand, Mingus closed her eyes and breathed. *Knock. Knock.* The initial relief of no answer grew unsettling after six knocks.

"M'Dea, it's me. Mingus. Let me in, please . . . I know what happened."

A key was under the back door mat. Mingus walked across the damp grass. As she neared the side gate, the front door cracked open behind her. A layer of tension peeled from her body. Car keys clutched to thigh, she walked back over to the front door and pushed it open with her fingertips—M'Dea was nowhere in sight.

Mingus placed her sandals next to her mother's plastic gardening boots outside the door and stepped in. The house smelled unfamiliar. She had crossed that threshold a thousand times; today seemed different. There was no pot roast or cornmeal fried catfish smell coming from the kitchen, but that wasn't it. Something else was missing.

"I'll be right out; I'm just getting out of the shower," M'Dea yelled from the hall bathroom. Her voice sounded normal. Maybe a tad more inflated than Mingus remembered.

She picked a piece of candy from the crystal dish on the end table. With both hands she rolled the tips of yellow cellophane between her thumb and index finger until the piece of butterscotch landed in her lap. She used to love butterscotch when she was a kid. Used to sneak two pieces to bed with her every night. Suck hard and slow until sleep came. Even now she didn't like sleeping, especially in bed. Something about the quiet and inactivity made her stir-crazy.

Mingus flipped the candy with her tongue as she looked around the room. Baby pictures and three-inch porcelain people lined the fireplace. She hadn't noticed them in years. Crystal animal figurines competed fiercely for space on maple-stained bookshelves. Her mother's knitting basket sat cozy in thick gray strings of carpet, two feet from her father's dingy green recliner. Mingus would have thought they were happy if she didn't know better. They'd been happy-looking for a long time, made her wonder how long the lie had been going on.

Eva's front-toothless, open-mouthed grin caught Mingus's gaze. She stared. Eva's eyes were still the same, almond-shaped teardrops that never fell. Her flat chest jutted out so far she looked uncomfortable. There must have been sixteen barrette-clipped ponytails in her hair. Mingus remembered the security of sitting between M'Dea's knees, playing with the small red and yellow rubberbands, while her hair was being twisted into the same style. She walked over to the console and picked up a picture of herself. She was wearing her favorite white lace Easter dress and narrow patent leather shoes. The shoes wrinkled when she walked, like the space above a frowning nose. She was five. Cute. But even approaching thirty, Mingus couldn't figure out what Eva saw in her back then that made her hate her so much. Whatever it was, it didn't disappear with time; Eva learned how to mask it better and Mingus pretended she had learned not to care.

"You want some lemonade?" M'Dea's voice trailed from the hallway into the kitchen.

"Yeah, I can get it," Mingus said, pushing up from the couch.

"No, you sit, I changed the cabinets around a few weeks ago. I'll be out in a second."

M'Dea was avoiding her. Mingus walked into the kitchen and leaned her shoulder against the doorframe. M'Dea had piled half a bag of cheese puffs onto a clear plastic tray. She stood at the counter, wiping her nose with a checkered dishtowel.

"M'Dea," Mingus said, watching the back of her mother's towel-covered head, waiting for her to turn around. M'Dea didn't say anything. Just grabbed the two glasses of lemonade and brushed past Mingus without making eye contact.

The cheese puffs were left sitting on the wood cutting board that extended from above the silverware drawer. Mingus didn't want any cheese puffs. M'Dea doesn't either, she thought. Mingus took the tray into the living room and placed it in the center of the coffee table atop the magazines. The tray sat between them: Mingus on the loveseat, her mother on the couch.

M'Dea reached over and grabbed one of the white linen napkins from the tray. She fluffed it with a single snap of wrist and let its triangular form drape her crossed knees.

"You came," she said, head lifted high, gaze falling just pass Mingus's right shoulder.

Mingus flinched. M'Dea's anger was perfectly articulated in her demeanor. The length of her erect spine, the intentional avoidance of Mingus's eyes. The subtleties of war are cruel, Mingus thought. She felt like a child again. Knowing she couldn't cross over because sides had been chosen a long time ago. Mingus was her father's child.

"I'm sorry about what happened, M'Dea, but please, don't take it out on me. I didn't know. I swear. I found out from Eva."

"Have you spoken to him?"

"I haven't talked to him in weeks."

Mingus watched her mother's eyes dart toward her and away.

"You usually take his side," M'Dea said.

"That's not true. It just seems like you always want me to choose."

"I make you choose?"

M'Dea looked her directly in the eye.

"Yeah," Mingus said, her voice turning soft. "It's like I can't love the both of you the same. Somebody always has to be loved more. And somebody always has to get their feelings hurt or the other one isn't happy. You guys do it to me and Eva both. Then we end up mad at each other."

"You chose your father because you love him m—"

"You don't believe that, M'Dea, I know you don't."

She looked deep into her mother's face. The hard lines that didn't soften around her tight jaw and nonblinking eyes said that she did mean it. Mingus swallowed the guilt in her throat.

"I don't love him more, M'Dea. I just think we get along better most of the time. Like you seem to get along better with Eva. And really, in the last few months, I haven't spoken much to either of you. I'm sorry about that. You know how hectic this time of year gets for me. Taking on new cases, working late nights at home. Only getting a few hours sleep, then starting over again."

M'Dea's squared-off frame matched the rigidity in her face. Mingus breathed hard through her mouth and found her gaze lowering into the gray strings of carpet. It wasn't work. It was Keith. It was everything that was supposed to be right and wasn't. It was taking work home at night because she couldn't concentrate during the day. It was her life falling apart and not wanting anyone to know about it.

Mingus scooted to the edge of the loveseat and leaned toward her mother. She spoke delicately, her words diffusing into the somberness of the room. "I love you, M'Dea. You're the only mother I have and I'm not here to take sides. I want to be here for the both of you."

With unspread fingers M'Dea systematically smoothed the imaginary wrinkles from her smock. Mingus knew where Eva got it from. The protective meanness.

"I don't deserve this, M'Dea. I know you're hurting, but you can't take this out on me. I didn't do this to you."

"Sometimes you can't have both. You try. You try to love two people the same and you can't." She paused. "It's nothing anyway. Your father's just going through a phase. That's all it is. It'll pass like everything else he's latched onto over the years."

"It *is* something," Mingus said, extending her hand to her mother's knee. "You can't pretend it's not."

M'Dea reached for the glass of lemonade closest to her on the table. She pursed her lips tightly around the rim as she drank, then lowered the glass to her lap.

Mingus felt an overwhelming sadness settle in her stomach. She looked at her mother in the faded pastel smock, a green-and-white striped towel wrapped around her head. She hadn't been in the shower. Her hair was parched.

Mingus lowered herself to the carpet and knelt on both knees in front of her. She unwrapped the towel from M'Dea's head. Red strands of hair fell stubbornly to her back. Mingus stared into her mother's eyes. They looked like storm clouds, twin clusters of gray, threatening rain at any moment.

"It's all right, M'Dea, it's all right."

Mingus took the glass of lemonade from M'Dea's lap and hugged her. She could feel heaving spread throughout her mother's chest. She hugged tighter. M'Dea fell into her like a stack of laundry that was piled too high. Tears dripped into Mingus's neck. M'Dea's sobs were heavy, like ripe fruit before it snaps from the vine. There was no turning back for either of them, not after a cry like that.

Punk Ass Nigga. Mingus felt like he had done it to her. Cheated on their relationship. They were close. Best friends. Mingus had never thought of her father in the same *no-count* fashion in which many women referred to their husbands and fathers. He was different. This was never supposed to happen to him.

M'Dea awoke from her daze when she felt tears melting onto her shoulder. Mingus cried for her mother, but more so she cried for herself: for not seeing the signs, for what her family had become, for being empty again. M'Dea grabbed the linen napkin from her lap and began to wipe Mingus's face.

"Shush," she said, blotting Mingus's eyes. "I didn't want you to have to go through this. That's why I told Eva not to tell you."

"What happened, M'Dea?"

"I don't know." M'Dea wiped her nose with the back of her hand. "I've tried so hard to figure it out. I just keep coming up with untouched meals.

"It was slow at first. 'I'm not hungry right now. Only a little bit,' he would say. Before I knew it, he was catching bites on the way home. Saying he had to work late. I was left with a refrigerator full of foil-covered meals and Carl was with another woman."

She made it sound so simple. Clean. Mingus sat on her knees looking up at her mother. She wanted to say something, tug at M'Dea's smock and ask some question that would help her understand. All that manifested was silence.

"Believe me, Mingus, I wondered what he did those nights. But every time questions popped into my head, reasons popped in right behind them. It's a new business. Endsbrook is forty miles outside of town. It made sense to me that Carl was on site a lot, at least until he hired an attendant—right?"

"I don't know," Mingus said, lips barely moving.

M'Dea flicked her middle finger against her thigh and took a deep breath.

"By the time the meals started piling up, it was too late. He often told me it was too late. Too late for sex. Too late for a movie. Too late for talking. It took everything in me to admit what was going on. It sounds crazy, but I could have accepted an affair. I just never thought he'd love someone else more than he loved m—"

"That's not right, Mama. How do you just accept another woman?"

Mingus plopped down Indian-style, letting her hair swing into her face. Stringy brown ringlets shielded her eyes from her mother's stare. M'Dea had a way of reading Mingus's mind when she looked into her eyes. And sometimes, like right then, Mingus didn't want to hurt her.

"You called me 'Mama.' "

Mingus sat on the floor looking at the strings of carpet gathered between her thighs. Water dripped from her nose and collected in the crevice between her lips.

"It's just nice to hear sometimes." M'Dea rested her hand on the top of Mingus's head. "That's what I used to call my mother. Mama."

Her nose was stopped-up. Mingus breathed slowly through her mouth to stop the aching in the back of her throat.

"This type of thing creeps up on you slow, Mingus," she said, smoothing the wildness of Mingus's hair. "You catch on at the end, when it's way too late. The little signs just make you hope the big ones never come. You make yourself think it's all in your head. It's never all in your head. Don't let anyone ever tell you that. You don't know your father, Mingus, not the way I know him. Your father and my husband are two different men, always have been."

Mingus raised her head, her eyes met with M'Dea's waist.

"Do you realize I've never had my own car? Thirty-five years and he's never mentioned me having my own transportation. He leaves the keys to that work truck *just in case* I need to go somewhere. I can't drive that big ole thing; he knows it. He doesn't even want me to. Just makes it seem like I have an option."

Mingus thought about the fact that whenever M'Dea came to visit her, her father dropped her off or she picked M'Dea up herself.

"I found the cards in the tool shed. One was from his birthday last year."

M'Dea closed her eyes to stop the tears from falling. They didn't stop. Tears rolled down her face and mixed with her words as she spoke:

" 'For my sweetheart on his birthday. Loving you has taught me so much. . . . You've shown me what it is to really care, how it feels to put another first. . . . With you I have learned so much about myself and my feelings. . . . With you I have discovered love. You have my heart, Me.' "

Mingus imagined M'Dea in the floral smock she'd been wearing for days straight, sitting in the dim light of the tool shed, reading intimacies written to her father by another woman. She felt helpless. M'Dea knew every word. Mingus wondered how many times she'd read it.

"She thinks she's smart. Signing everything 'Me.' Her name is Glenda."

The saliva had dried up in Mingus's mouth. She reached over her shoulder for a glass of lemonade. The ice cubes were melting into smooth glassy ovals. Mingus drank it, imagining it was vodka.

"I found her business card in his glove compartment. Four or five of them. You know how he throws stuff in there. One of them had her home number and 'call me' on the back. Same handwriting as the birthday card. 'Glenda Stewart, Lexus sales representative.' Glenda."

"Glenda," Mingus said quietly, seeing what her name felt like on her tongue. It tasted soft but bland. She had expected a name with sting like Sybil, or Rhoda, or Eva, for that matter.

M'Dea leaned back into the couch and hugged a burgundy-and-blue striped pillow into her stomach.

"All I can do is ask myself what she has that I don't. What she looks like. What color her hair is. What color *she* is."

M'Dea stared at Mingus with an odd awareness. She'd never looked at her that way before.

"I don't want her to be black, Mingus," M'Dea said, looking Mingus dead in the eye, seeming sad for having to say it. "She could be anything. Chinese. Indian. I just don't want her to be black."

Mingus wished she would have said something to calm her mother's fears—"Color doesn't matter . . . an affair is an affair . . . don't blame yourself for his mistake"—but she didn't. One thing popped into her head.

"You should divorce him, M'Dea," she said, her voice cracking. "I can write the petition. We can start compiling a comprehensive list of assets. You already have tangible proof, layered with the fact that you're a dependent spouse and you've been married for thirt—"

"Shh."

"Let me help you," Mingus said, tears starting to well in her eyes again.

"Come here."

M'Dea patted the cushion next to her with her left hand. Mingus noticed the worn wedding band on her finger. There was no engagement ring.

"I appreciate you wanting to help me, really, but I'm not going to let you do this. This is between your father and me. You're not in the middle, you understand? I'm sorry if I've made you feel that way. It wasn't my intention."

Mingus nodded. She was in the middle.

"And I'm fifty-three years old. I'm not sure divorce is the answer for me anyway. I'm used to being a wife—taking care of my kids, cooking meals, making sure the house runs properly."

"Eva and I have been gone for over ten years. Dad's not here. There's nobody for you to take care of anymore. You have to think about yourself now. This house is dead. And you can't live your life for a house or for a family that's not here."

"That's not true," she said, her voice thick with conviction. "Eva just moved out again two and a half months ago. She stops by a lot. Your dad comes through. And I like it here, this is my home."

"I'm not telling you to give it up. But I am telling you to understand every single penny it takes to support it. I meet women like you all the time, M'Dea. Their husbands earn all the money, pay the major bills. Invest. Dad owns and leases out several real estate properties. I bet you don't even know what they net or how much they're worth."

M'Dea took her hand from Mingus's lap.

"Look," Mingus said, "I'm not downing you. I appreciate everything you've done for me. I mean that. But you have to protect yourself. And I'm not saying that Daddy would screw you, but just as often as I meet women who are trying to learn about the holdings of their estates and their husbands' businesses, I also meet their husbands who are wanting to liquefy assets and set up untouchable accounts."

"It's not important to me, Mingus. I've survived this long."

Mingus got back down on her knees and held both of M'Dea's hands between hers.

"That's fine, M'Dea. That's fine. I just want you to know your rights. If you don't want the information right now, just give me authorization and let me check Dad's—"

M'Dea pulled her hands away.

"Do you hear yourself? Plotting and carrying on? That is your father. And I'm not leaving my marriage, Mingus, and that's that."

"So, you're just going to stay here and let him hurt you like this?"

"Shhh."

"I can help yo—"

"Shhh."

M'Dea motioned to her and pulled Mingus into her chest. Mingus pushed away.

"I have to go to the bathroom."

She locked the door behind her and sat on the toilet with the lid down. The cramps were coming back; this time near her spine. She tried to breathe deeply, but surges of anger and hurt cut her breath short. She needed some air. The bathroom felt tiny with all the emotions floating around inside her. Mingus looked at the wall in front of her. It was perfectly white. No smudge marks around the light switch, no dirt. The standing ashtray next to the toilet had no ash. That's when she noticed what was missing. It wasn't fried food or freshly cut flowers; it was the cigar smoke. Her nose finally caught on. Daddy is gone.

Chapter 2

I didn't know how to tell Mingus about the videotape. How my hands shake. How I feel a dull ache around my heart each time I think about it and I haven't even seen it yet. It's under the mattress on my side of the bed. I feel it poking me in the back when I sleep. Most nights, I sit up in the kitchen. Drink a few cups of decaf and stare at the black plastic cover on the table in front of me. Sip, stare, and wonder.

I've tried so hard to convince myself it's nothing, but how could it be? It was in the tool shed with the birthday card and letters. Call it women's intuition, but there was something about the way Carl had hidden it. In a gasoline tin. The kind you use when you run out of gas. He'd cut a metal rectangle out of the back and placed it against the wall, on the shelf with cleaning agents and wood varnishes.

My first few times in the tool shed, I didn't notice it. But on the third time, after I'd already found the letters, it stuck out to me. A spanking new gas tin on the shelves with grubby, soil-covered bottles and cans. The yellow flag across the front said Millin's Gas. I don't know a Millin's Gas on our side of town.

The letters were in a drawer. Wrapped in an old army bag with his faded initials on it, behind a red metal box of ratchet tools. Maybe he knew I was coming. That it was only a matter of time before I made my way out of the house and into the shed. And all I keep thinking is—at least he could have locked it. With the silver padlock that dangles from the door. The one I don't know the combination to. Carl could have protected me from this. If I didn't have the tape, the letters, the lipstick, I could convince myself this wasn't happening. I could miss him right, like a woman is supposed to miss her husband. I wouldn't have to be mad at myself. I wouldn't feel stuck. I wouldn't be sitting here, wondering what kind of woman wears Tender Chocolate.

Chapter 3

June 4

It's hard for me to think of my mother as white. She's always been M'Dea. Somehow, that just made her human.

Hands tight on the steering wheel, Mingus drifted into the slow lane.

She kept thinking about what M'Dea had said—Anything but black. Chinese. Indian. Anything but black. It shocked Mingus, that after thirty-five years of marriage to a black man and raising a black family, a black woman was what M'Dea feared most.

Growing up there were no black women. Mingus thought everyone had a white mom. White mothers held little moist hands and walked their children to school. Picked them up. Attended parent conferences and PTA meetings. Mingus knew that white mothers were normal. Her neighborhood experiences told her that. Black daughters were the ones who were different. The broken rhythm of lying hellos and too-long stares made her brownness feel wrong in her mother's hand. Made her wish for hair with less kinky curl and temporary tans. Wish that the same women who looked at her mother with disgust would one day want to be her friends.

Mingus never talked about it, but she wanted a best friend more than anything, someone besides her diary to tell all her secrets to. She would play tetherball with little white girls on asphalt courts. Hang upside down with them on metal rings in sandboxes with thick concrete borders. They knew her name and she knew theirs. They'd even share the same crayon box during coloring time. But Mingus knew. These friendships were makeshift, lasting only from the Pledge of Allegiance to the dismissal bell.

Her family was the anomaly in the neighborhood. The family folks might wave to but never invite her over for dinner. Sometimes Mingus would settle with herself: If she couldn't have a best friend, maybe all she needed was a birthday party. A big one, with pin-the-tail-on-the-donkey and bobbing for apples. She wanted to stand in front of a lit birthday cake with a sea of small, shiny faces surrounding her. Everyone would have a cone hat on their head, a red and green blowout or kazoo in their mouth. Instead, she had her father to talk to, and intimate birthdays comprising cake, ice cream, pizza, and family.

Mingus angled the rearview mirror toward her face. Her skin was the color of yellow sunshine mixed with hints of red and brown. Freckles bridged both sides of her nose. Her nose. It was a black nose—soft, round edges. Her lips. They were black lips—full like the flesh of a peeled ripe orange.

Do I look like the enemy my mother sees in her dreams? she asked herself. The answer was inherent in the question. She watched as her reflection fell apart. Watched like it was someone else's eyes crowding with heavy-bottomed tears. She felt sorry for the person staring back at her. The person who longed for simpler times like when her classmates called her chocolate. Like before any of them knew what a half-breed nigger was.

An intense thud shot through Mingus's chest. She hadn't seen the car in front of her. Mingus crossed the solid white line and parked on the side of the road. She watched as a thirty-something white man in khaki walking shorts and a beige button-down shirt came barging toward her.

"See what you did?" he said, pointing back to his car. "It's people like you who shouldn't have licenses."

"Black people?" Mingus blurted out before she realized what she had said.

"What are you talking about? You just rode my tail for over a mile."

"I didn't see you—I'm sorry." She bit the inner flesh of her lower lip and quickly wiped her fingers across her eyes. Her purse was on the passenger seat. Mingus pulled two cards from her wallet and passed them through the half-opened window. "Here's my insurance information; here's my license."

Her insurance card was dented with the imprint of wet fingers. He took the cards from her and handed her his.

"You didn't see me?"

"No," she said.

He glanced at her license then looked into her eyes. "Are you okay?"

"I'm fine."

"No, I mean are you *okay?* You seem shaken up pretty badly."

Mingus stared back at him.

"I'm fine."

He wrote her information on a small notepad and squatted next to the car.

"Ms. Browning, I think it's fair that I tell you I'm a police officer, and you don't look fine. Fortunately, this was a minor incident. But you have to be more careful. When you're emotionally distressed, especially to the point where you don't see a three-ton vehicle in front of you, you need to exit the freeway and sit in a shopping center or restaurant parking lot until you regain composure. You're a beautiful young lady but every time you drive in this state, you're not only endangering yourself, you're endangering everyone who happens to be in your proximity."

Mingus watched his mouth move in soundless slow motion. When his forehead tensed with conviction, she nodded. When he smiled, she smiled back.

"You live on Marisol Drive, correct?"

"Yes."

"That's not far away, do you think you'll be able to make it home?"

"I'll be fine."

"Well, take some deep breaths and settle yourself before you start driving."

He stood up and tapped the hood of the car.

Mingus nodded, released the parking brake, and drove off in second gear.

She locked the dead bolt behind her and slid off her jogging shorts and sandals. The air was still muggy. Mingus pulled the T-shirt over her head and walked across the living room to open a window. Wood warmed the bottom of her feet. French lace tickled her face in the breeze. The lace reminded her of the game she and Eva used to play when their father would send them off to bed. Instead of going straight to sleep, Mingus would lie in the center of the bed, arms outstretched, and Eva would jump as high and as close to Mingus as possible without hitting her. Sometimes, the ruffles at the bottom of Eva's gown would whisk past Mingus, tickling her face. Never once did Eva hit her. Mingus missed that. The assurance of knowing she could trust Eva.

She reflected on the fact that Eva stopped wanting to play the game all of a sudden. Sleep time came. Mingus took off her slippers and lay in the center of the bed with her arms outstretched as usual.

"You wanna play Eva?"

Eva stood there, channeling annoyance, hands on her bony ten-year-old hips. She never answered Mingus's question, just pushed Mingus over to her side of the bed, turned her back, and told

Mingus to go to sleep. Mingus didn't think much of it. She knew Eva was moody. But in less than a month, Eva convinced M'Dea that she was too old to share a bedroom with a five-year-old. She needed more space. More quiet time to get her studies done. For her eleventh birthday she got a new bedroom set, and for the first time, Mingus realized she hated sleeping alone.

Mingus stared out of the window into the overgrown field in front of her apartment building. As much as she needed someone to confide in, she realized. Eva wasn't going to act better and Keith wasn't coming back. She pulled a legal notepad and colored marker from under the couch and started to brainstorm places to meet eligible black men. She had come up with the grocery store, Black Lawyer's Society meetings, and church, which she wasn't a member of, before the phone rang.

"Hello."

"Is this Mingus Browning?"

The voice didn't sound familiar.

"I'm sorry, she's not available," Mingus said, propping the phone between her ear and shoulder. "Would you like to leave a message?"

"Oh yeah, of course. My name is Steven Reynolds, I met her earlier today."

The only person she'd met was the police officer.

"This is Mingus Browning."

"Screening your calls, huh?"

"What can I do for you?"

"You sound quite a bit better than you did earlier today."

She pressed the balls of her feet against the beveled edge of the coffee table.

"Thank you. What can I do for you?"

"Listen, I'm not even going to pretend I'm calling under the pretext of the accident. I saw you, thought you were attractive, didn't see a wedding ring, and since we were both having a less than perfect day, I was hoping we could get together for dinner or drinks and have a better evening."

Mingus tapped her foot on the edge of the table a few times.

"How did you get my phone number? It's not on my insurance card."

"You're listed."

"There are three M. Brownings in the book."

"I tried two," he said.

She bit the inside of her bottom lip and tried not to smile.

"Mr. Reynolds, Steven, thank you for your interest. You seem like a nice enough guy, really, but I don't date white boys. No offense."

"Don't or haven't."

"Both."

"Believe me, I don't mean to sound cocky or anything, but I haven't been a boy for a long time and you don't seem like a little girl. I'm talking about conversation, dinner, and no strings. Maybe we'll even have fun."

"Again, thank you, but I'm in for the rest of the night."

"All right, I'll bow out gracefully then."

"Have a good night."

Lowering the phone, she could hear him calling her name.

"Yes," she said, the phone raised back to her ear.

"Are you familiar with Giovanni's on Derby Street?"

"I am."

"Should you change your mind, I'll be dining there tonight at eight o'clock."

He had to be out of his mind. She smiled. Something in her liked the way he said her name. Honest. Almost innocent. She cringed. He had no idea what he was asking of her—to endure the same social crucifixion her parents had endured their entire lives together. She'd witnessed it her whole life.

I'm really tired tonight and I've had a long day, she said to herself. She glanced at the alarm clock on the desk and noticed the crystal bud vase with a dead red rose curled over its rim. It had been dead for over a month. The rosy scent had completely dried up. The leaves folded into themselves. Mingus stared soberly at the rose, feeling a kindredness—how long before her petals would start to fall?

Chapter 4

She hasn't said anything yet. Just messed with them damn house plants. Trimming leaves, watering, changing soil. I tell you, nothing was wrong with them plants. She stood over my shoulder damn near the whole first inning of the baseball game. Justa clipping away. I'd look up and she'd give me that calm, don't-close-your-eyes-while-I-have-these-scissors-in-my-hand stare. I couldn't even watch the rest of the game. Told her, "Elaine, I'm going out to the tool shed to work on them shelves for that book-case." "You do that," she told me back, just as calm. You do that.

If men are lacking in the intuition department, I don't know what you call the pain that struck me smack between my eyes. She musta found the letters, I thought. It scared me, that Elaine might know for sure I had another woman, but that's the most peace I've had in two years. At least if she knew she wouldn't have to wonder no more. I wouldn't have to lie. It's downright painful the way she looks at me. Always asking me why, with every hello, every time I pick up my keys to leave.

I feel heavy around her. Like there's a thirty-something-year-old weight on my shoulders. When it comes down to it, all we have is them years. It'll be thirty-five in August. But can't nobody live their life in the past. She's always talking about how good it used to be. Used to be can't make me happy right now. Used to be don't fill the emptiness I felt lying next to her. It's too painful. Can't neither one of us sleep in that bed no more.

Reality is, when I think back on the past, best thing I remember is the birth of my girls. Eva came out of the womb screaming at the top of her lungs. Mingus was as quiet as dew collecting on grass. Doctor had to spank her bottom just to get a whimper out of her. Part of me expected that since our first child was a girl, Mingus was definitely going to be a boy. I had prayed for a boy. Somebody I could raise to be different than me. I wanted my boy to be free like water. Never staying in one place unless he wanted to. Getting to travel the world. Marrying somebody who looked like him. I don't blame Ellie, but there's something wrong with not being able to go to the grocery store with your wife. Being a real estate broker and having your wife purchase your house in her name because you know a black man isn't welcomed in the neighborhood unless he's the gardener. Something's wrong when protecting your family means putting yourself behind them because being in front could get someone hurt.

When I walked up on the tool shed, I could tell Ellie'd been in there. The door was left partially open. I rolled out the bottom storage drawer, unfolded my old army bag. The letters were gone. Shoulda locked it, but damn, Elaine don't ever go out to the tool shed. She'd already searched my trunk and glove compartment. My side of the closet. I'd know 'cause little things would be missing. Business cards, receipts, matchbooks. Got to the point where I'd throw everything away, even a beer receipt, for fear of her finding some small piece of evidence in my pant pocket.

I couldn't throw the letters away though. I ain't never had a woman make me feel powerful just by writing how she feels about me. Glenda makes me feel—like things are gone be all right. She know I ain't perfect and don't expect me to be. She says every man got a wandering eye, even the best ones, that's why a woman got to handle her business right. And when a woman handles her business, a man is gone fall in line every time.

With Elaine having the letters, I didn't know how to go back in the house. Part of me wanted to wait her out. I milled about the tool shed and found some old music I used to mess around with when I was younger. Back in those days I took pride in lining the staffs myself. Used to use the Bible my mama gave me. The big burgundy hardback kind that had pages inside to record the birth dates, marriages, and baptisms of your children. Used to open the Bible flat on a blank page and use a black pen to make five perfectly straight lines. Then I'd carve up the tip of a pencil with my pocket knife and mark in the notes. Always felt closer to God after writing in music, like if we didn't have nothing else in common, the music would bind us.

I flipped over a milk crate and thumbed through the curled pages. "Ain't That a Shame," "Night Train," "September in the Rain"—*The leaves of brown came tumbling down, remember, in September, in the rain.*

Man, it's amazing to me that I remembered the words to those old songs, the melodies, even without looking at the notes. Du du du du du du—Doo, doo, doo, doo, doo. "Harlem Nocturne" had to be one of my favorites. The music got me so excited, man, I had no choice but to take out my saxophone. Pulled the case from my bottom left drawer and put it together. Secured my reed. It sounded rusty—really, I sounded rusty. It'd been a long time since I messed with that saxophone. Ellie used to get nervous every time she heard me playing. Like I was one step closer to the door. She called it right. Music used to get me going in the right direction. And the right direction always led away from her.

I popped in a tape of "Let My Children Hear Music" I

recorded from the LP. Unplugged the headphones from my Walkman and tipped up the sound. Rewound it to the first track. "The Shoes of the Fisherman's Wife Are Some Jive-Ass Slippers." I sat there on the milk crate with my sax strapped around my neck, tapping my foot in time, listening to the slow roll of the saxophone and bass in unison, traveling through the heart of what hurt is. I listened while the music rolled from pain to melancholy joy into steady laughter and back again. I imagined me and Charles on the bandstand fighting for the music. Living in the music. And I just played. Hitting every wild and sharp note my life never would. Played like my breath depended on it. Rewound and played it over and over and over again.

After while, when my shirt and trousers were heavy with sweat and I had worked myself out good, that's when I checked on the videotape. Wasn't no way in God's green kingdom she coulda found that tape. I pushed the milk crate against the storage counter and stepped up to grab the oil can off the shelf. Nothing moved around when I shook it. I stepped down off the crate and looked in.

She had no right. I had hid that tape so nobody could find it except me and God. Bought a new gas can. Cut a perfect rectangle out the back. Stuck it against the wall on the top shelf. Knowing something is one thing; seeing is another. Wasn't no way Elaine was gonna watch that tape. I wasn't gone let her.

Chapter 5

June 6
Sometimes when I was little, I used to wonder
what it would have been like to have a brown
family. Now I wonder if M'Dea ever wished for
a white one.

It was the habit of remembering that made her fear. Of being dressed in a pink chiffon strapless dress her mother had sewn. Hair straightened shiny with a hot comb and feathered over the right eye. It was having a boutonniere chilling in the refrigerator for the first time. It was her mother's perfume on her neck and Eva's laughter. It was waiting at the window for Jeremy Cohen who didn't show and whose phone call came too late.

Mingus sat at the bar sipping a cherry 7UP, eating an occasional salted peanut. She could barely remember the color of his hair, more less what he looked like. Shit, she thought, another free meal with no future attached.

She looked down the bar. There seemed to be an empty stool at the very end. A dark corner is less conspicuous, she assured herself. She didn't want to be on interracial date display. That was always the hardest part about family outings. People thinking that the four of them were fair game because they dared to come out in public together. Sometimes Mingus used to think that there should have been a special dining cage in restaurants for biracial families. They could arrive, check their coats, and sit on a raised stage in the center of the restaurant for the duration of their appearance. As the family ate, people could gawk and turn their chairs to get a better view. Occasionally, a grandmother could reach through the bars and stroke the father's black fingers or the child's hair. By the end of the evening, all curiosities would be satisfied and the family could go home. Knowing that next time, there would be a new group of greedy onlookers awaiting.

Mingus placed her handbag over her shoulder and walked through the crowd, holding the glass of 7UP close to her chest. With each step, her dress inched up her thighs. She pulled the dress knee level and sat down. "I shouldn't have worn this thing," she said into her glass and took a small piece of ice into her mouth.

"You all right, sistah?"

His voice was baritone smooth. Dots of warmth pricked her cheeks.

"I'm fine," Mingus said, taking a quick glance at the man seated next to her. Ice turned to water on her tongue. Of all the seats in the bar, she had to choose one next to a brother. She placed her purse on her lap and pulled the hem of the dress so that it covered her knees.

"Stop tugging on that dress," he said smiling, lowering what looked like cranberry juice onto a black napkin. "You look fine."

"Thank you," she said.

Their eyes locked. His right cheek dimpled.

"Eric," he said, right hand extended.

"Mingus," she said back.

Her attention shifted to the meeting of their skin. She watched as the smallness of her hand got swallowed by the pink flesh of his palm. The firmness of her handshake softened into his. Mingus pulled away.

"I have to go. It's been good meeting you," she said.

She looked down into her purse and unsnapped a small change pouch. She laid two dollars on the counter under her empty glass. As she was about to get up, hands squeezed the outside of her bare shoulders.

"Looks like I got here just in time," Steven said.

"Looks like," she said, trying to smile.

"That dress looks fantastic on you. Black's definitely your color."

In the corner of her eye she could see the brother staring at her. She turned toward Steven.

"Well, I'm hoping the fact that you're here this evening means you're taking me up on dinner."

"I wouldn't be here if I wasn't," she smiled, feeling eyes on the back of her neck.

"Beautiful. I'll go check on our table. You can sit here till I get back if you like."

"I'll come with."

Steven held out his hand to help her down from the barstool.

"Have a good evening, sistah," the brother said in an unrushed fashion. Mingus, hand in Steven's, turned and nodded.

Bluesy midtempo jazz played backdrop to Mingus's thoughts. She tapped her fingers on the edge of the wine menu, occasionally rolling her shoulders in time. She imagined what it would be like. Being seated next to her mother in the courtroom. The judge announcing the next case on the docket. Number four, *Browning* vs. *Browning.* She would stand to face the judge as Mingus Browning Esq., representing the plaintiff Elaine Browning against her own father. The whole thing sounded heartbreaking. Reality was, she didn't want to defend her mother. Not against her father. Her willingness exposed a fault line in her faithfulness. They were supposed to be closer than this. He'd always told Mingus the truth about everything. Even if he had to code the language, the look would tell her what he couldn't speak. Or maybe it was the way he held a certain kind of breath or how his eyes rolled. She should have found this out from him. Not from Eva. Not M'Dea. Him. But work is work and wrong is wrong, she thought. She would turn off her heart muscle just like she had to do in any other case. He would have to understand, like she had to understand.

"You know," Steven said, "a good Zinfandel would go great with your scampi. The fruitiness always opens up my taste buds."

"I'm just browsing. Cranberry juice is fine."

"You can have both, all I have to do is flag down our waitress. It wouldn't be a problem."

She glanced up from the menu and caught his smile fading into a subtle grin.

"Thank you," she said.

"So, I was surprised to see you tonight. What made you change your mind?"

"Honest?"

"Of course," he said.

Mingus thought about breaking down the whole reason but changed her mind.

"I was curious."

Steven kept eye contact while taking a couple sips of wine.

"Curious because?"

Mingus leaned in toward the crystal candelabra in the middle of the table. Steven followed suit. The votive flame accentuated the green flecks in his eyes.

"Tell me something," she said, asking more with her eyes than her voice, "have you ever done this before?"

"I've dated lots of different types of women. Latin, Asian, I—"

"You know what I'm talking about."

"No," he said.

"No, not seriously or not ever?"

"No, as in this is my first date."

Mingus broke a breadstick in half and placed it on the saucer in front of her. Steven took the other half from the basket and bit into it.

"Interesting," she said.

"Why is that?" He covered his mouth with his hand as he chewed.

"Well, for what, thirty-some-odd years you've never dated a black woman and now in some strange twist of happenings you're on your first interracial date and it's with me. That doesn't sound interesting to you?"

"Because this is my first date doesn't mean this is the first time I've wanted to. I just never have."

"Why now?" she said.

Steven licked the garlic butter from his fingers.

"Is there a reason you're interrogating me or is this just your style?"

"I'm a lawyer, what do you expect?"

"But you're also a woman. So what I want to know is, who is asking the questions—the woman or the lawyer?"

His smile caught her off guard. She rolled the tip of a breadstick in alfredo sauce and bit into it.

"The woman is asking."

Steven rubbed his palms together.

"Now we are getting somewhere," he said.

"Who has the linguine and clams?"

The waitress held a round platter with four plates on her flat palm.

"I do," Steven said, unbuttoning his sports jacket but still staring at Mingus.

"Miss, here's your scampi."

"Thank you."

Mingus pushed the bread saucer to the side of the table.

"Can I get anything else for you, more breadsticks?"

Mingus shook her head no. "We're fine, thank you," Steven said.

Glancing away, Mingus noticed the brother she'd met at the bar being led to his table. He followed behind a woman in a short peach skirt suit with long, oiled legs. Mingus's eyes followed behind him. She tried not to stare, but couldn't help it. His skin was the color of pecans roasted in a dark brown sugar glaze. A goatee framed his black plum lips. She wanted to lick them.

"Thinking about something?" Steven said in a comfortable tone.

Mingus sipped her cranberry juice.

"Nothing particular."

"I asked you out because of timing," he said as if he'd been pondering the reason. "I thought you were attractive, I liked your wild hair, and I wanted to get into something tonight."

Mingus gathered pasta around her fork and twisted it against the spoon until the noodles resembled a tightly woven spool of thread.

"I'm out with you tonight," she paused, checking Steven's facial expression, "because despite telling myself and you that I wasn't coming, I found myself searching my closet for something to wear, then finding shoes, then pulling my hair into a chignon, and before I knew it, I was halfway here."

"Whew," he said cracking his knuckles with a big smile on his face. "It's nice to know I still have it."

Mingus folded her arms over her chest.

"So this is about your notch card," she said.

"Not hardly. It took everything I had to ask you out. You made my week. Month."

She rolled her eyes.

"*Um hmph.*"

"What's that supposed to mean?"

Mingus leaned into the table.

"It's a sistah thing," she said with sass.

Steven smiled.

"Okay, sister."

"What did you say?"

"Sister. Okay, sister . . . what?"

She couldn't help but laugh.

"I've never heard a white person call me *sistah* before."

"Well, what if I told you I've never called anyone *sister* before, not in that sense."

"What sense is that?"

His cheeks blushed.

"You know, in an African-American cultural camaraderie sense."

"You're something else," she said.

"I take that as a compliment."

Mingus became aware of the smile spreading across her lips. It was one of those honest smiles that had nothing to do with niceties or pretense. She took a fork full of pasta into her mouth and chewed slowly, trying to remember the last time she was really happy. She couldn't remember.

"You want to talk about it?"

"Come again?"

"That's the same look you had on your face when I met you earlier. I knew something was wrong but I didn't want to invade your privacy."

Mingus stared hard into his eyes. She liked the way he didn't turn away.

"Can I be honest?"

"Of course," he said.

"I'm half-white. My whole life I've lived as a black person. From hair products to men. Part of me came here tonight just to see if I was missing anything."

He smiled a little, then leaned back in his chair.

"I kinda got that," he said.

Instinctively the space between her eyebrows wrinkled.

"What do you mean, you kind of got it?"

"I mean, there had to be something besides my charm that got you here. You were adamant about the fact that you didn't date *white boys*—never had and didn't desire to. I didn't expect you to come. When you did, I figured it was about some sort of notch on *your* belt."

Mingus dropped her fork to her plate.

"You have to be kidding."

"Hey, I know how you women can be. 'Yeah girl, I had that white boy wrapped around my finger. Even had him looking through the white pages to get my number.'"

Mingus laughed.

"You have lost your mind," she said.

He raised his brows.

"Don't forget our police force is thirty-five percent black. You'd be surprised what I hear day to day."

"*Umph,*" Mingus said, shaking her head, still smiling, "You can think that if you want to, but a notch is about sex and we both know I am not trying to have sex with you tonight."

"Usually sex." He swallowed hard and chased his food with a shot of lemon water. "But a notch can be gained from anything. Sex, a phone number, being out with a beautiful woman and being seen, getting her back to your place for coffee, getting back to her place. Anything."

"Seems like you have it down to a science."

"Actually, I don't get out much."

"*Pleeasse,*" she said, tempted to roll her eyes.

"No, seriously, I'm not shitting you. The police force has strange deployment periods. A Friday or Saturday off is a rare commodity."

"You know a black woman dating a white police officer is an oxymoron, don't you?"

"Kind of like a Christian dating Beelzebub?"

"Basically," she said.

Steven put down his glass.

"Don't tell me you're one of those who believes the *white man* is the devil?"

"If I believed that, I would also have to believe that my white mother is the devil."

Steven leaned back in his chair again.

"I was raised by my father, also a police officer, Milwaukee though. He used to tell me stories about my mother when I was little. I used to wonder what it would have been like to know her. Sometimes I still do. But that's a whole different conversation."

Steven took a long drink of water. Mingus followed suit with cranberry juice. A part of her wondered what had happened to his mother, but another part of her didn't want to know.

"Are you and your mother close?" he said, after a few moments.

"She and my sister are closer."

"You ever wonder if she loves your sister more?"

Mingus circled her finger around the top of her empty glass.

"Sometimes. But I've just always been closer to my father."

"A daddy's girl." He smiled. "That's how I want my daughter to be. If I have a daughter. But I decided a long time ago that I would only have one. Whatever it is, I don't want my child to feel like it has to compete with anyone else for my attention."

"Your father remarried?" Mingus said.

"No. But he's been with the same woman for about twenty years. They have two kids together. One's nineteen, one's eleven."

He stared at her from across the table.

"What?" she said.

"Just admiring you. You look more like your mom or dad?"

"My mom's eyes, my dad's nose and lips, neither of their color."

He continued staring.

"Now that I think about it, you do have that kind of biracial look to you."

"Is that why you asked me out?"

"Come on, Mingus. I asked you out because I thought you were beautiful. Nothing scientific or racial to it."

"Sorry. I think I'm just sensitive today. And something about dating and relationships makes me overanalytical."

"Been burned?"

"Burned, chopped up, souffléd. You name it, I've been there."

"Divorced?"

"No, praise God. You?" she said.

"Yep. I was married for all of two years."

"What happened?"

"I probably wasn't really ready and neither was she. We ended up making a bad shot of it."

Mingus nodded, then instinctively buried her attention into her cold scampi.

"It's clear I hit a nerve; did I say something wrong?"

"It's nothing." Methodically she maneuvered the four prongs of her fork between two sticking noodles, separating them from each other. "I'm just sick of people giving up on their commitments then giving excuses for why their relationships don't work."

"That's not what I'm trying to do. But the reality is that some people don't belong together."

"You sound like my sister." She darted a look, then recommitted her attention to her food.

"Listen to me. Divorce is actually harder than being married to the person. At least marriage does have some good parts, however small they may be. With divorce, it takes a lot of time to even start seeing what's good about it. All I felt for the first two years afterward was the disappointment of it not working. Then your mind plays this strange game on you and tries to make you think it wasn't as bad as you know it was and that maybe you should go back. But in your heart you know you shouldn't."

Mingus thought about the fact that she had told M'Dea to divorce her father.

"Do you think it's ever one person's fault?" she asked.

"I don't know." He shook his head. "I think it gets way more complicated than whose fault it is. It's always easier to blame and say it would have worked better if she would have let me into her head more or knew how to stand by me. But it didn't happen that way, and I'd be the first person to admit it's hard being married to a cop. The crazy hours, the stress, the wondering on the daily basis if I'm going to make it home again." He smiled. "I'm not scaring you away am I?"

"It's not you. This topic just gets me worked up and I really don't want to get worked up right now."

Mingus removed her napkin from her lap and placed it over her plate.

"You're not going to hold it against me, are you?"

"What do you mean?"

"Meaning, when I ask you out again, you're not going to brush me off, right?"

"No," she said, "I'm not." Her smile was sad and reflective. "I had a good time with you tonight. Thank you."

"You're very welcome. You know, this restaurant has the best strawberry flan this side of Italy."

"Not tonight."

"You can take it to go."

"I'm going to pass," she said, pushing her chair out from under the table. "It's been a long day; I better get going."

"I'll walk you out."

Her feet were nervous. Mingus stood facing Steven, her behind touching the driver's side window, her left hand grasping the door handle behind her.

"It was good meeting you," she said, nervously extending her right hand.

He raised it to his lips. A soft flash of warmth stung her skin.

"Good meeting you as well."

It was subtle. Visibly she couldn't see the change, but something in her felt the air liquefying to heat between them and Steven moving closer.

"You know what, I really have to go to the ladies' room."

"Oh," he said taking a small step back, "I could walk you back in."

"No, you've been more than a gentleman. I'll be fine."

"Are you sure?"

"Yeah," she said. "I'm gonna pop back in and then I'll be on my way."

"Monday, maybe we could set something up?"

"That might work. Call me."

"Will do."

When she finished, Mingus paused at the pay phone. She stood with two coins in her hand, contemplating whether or not to call. Maybe she shouldn't have said what she said. It had been thirty-five years. Maybe M'Dea knew what she was talking about. Maybe not. "Whew." She closed her eyes and let out a breath that left heaviness in her chest.

"You're not giving up on us, sistah," she heard in her periphery.

"Excuse me," Mingus said, opening her eyes, craning her neck to the left.

"I hope you haven't given up on us." He smoothed his goatee between his thumb and index finger. "Sometimes brothahs aren't handling our business and it puts sistahs in the position of having to look elsewhere for what they should be getting at home."

"Well, excuse me, you don't know me and my personal life is none of your business."

Mingus dropped her change into the phone slot and immediately hung up.

"Is there a problem?" she asked, sensing his eyes still on her.

He smiled, and the dimple appeared again on his right cheek.
"Nothing we can't fix," he said, still smiling.

"Is this how you normally start a conversation?"

"I say what's on my mind."

She stared at him, amazed that she could have such an adverse reaction to such a fine-ass brother.

"One thing, and I'll leave you to your evening."

"And?" she said.

"Try loving a brother, you might like it."

He reached into his jacket and handed her his card.

"Ain't that about nothing," she said under her breath as she watched him exit through the double doors. Thoughts of Superfly popped into her mind. Mingus crumpled his card into her change purse and dialed M'Dea. The answering machine picked up. "Hey M'Dea, it's me. I just wanted to talk to you about the conversation we had earlier. Tell you I love you. I stepped out for a while, but I'm heading home now. You're probably asleep; I'll call you to-morrow."

Chapter 6

I watched him from the dining room. Watched him shut the tool shed door tight and clasp the combination lock. It'd been a long time since he'd opened that lock. I stood hunched over at the window, looking through a corner of the blinds. Carl turned the barrel back and forth until the lock finally clicked open. I couldn't hear the click, but I could see the victory. That I'll-fix-her expression on his face. He slipped the metal U-prong through holes in the door lever—the shed was locked. Simple. And he was too late. I already knew what I didn't want to know.

I sat down at the kitchen table with a bowl of green beans I had pulled from the garden. Laid a kitchen towel across my lap and started to snap. Snapped off the pointed brown tips. Snapped them into inch-long pieces. The screen door opened. Then the sliding glass. He walked toward me. His slacks grazed the table edge.

"Give me the tape."

His eyes were barely opened slits. Tight black eyes focused on me.

"What tape?" I said, taking more green beans from the bowl and laying them in my lap.

"Cut the shit, Elaine; I want my tape."

"Don't you mean *our* tape. Our marriage, our house—our tape."

"You have no right to go through my shit. I bought this house. Give me the tape, Elaine."

"What do you prove when you say that to me? Huh? Yes, your money bought this house and it doesn't make it any less mine. You know why? Because I am your wife. Not some tramp you've been screwing for the last thirty-five years. I cook your meals, I raised our children, I clean the damn toilets in this house. You can't pull rank on me, Carl. I'm entitled to half of everything we have if not more."

He pushed the table forward with his leg, tipping it into my stomach, knocking some beans from my lap. I slid the chair back with my feet and stayed seated.

"What, Carl? You gonna hit me now? Is that tape worth so much you'd hurt me over it?"

"You have no right." His voice raised, both hands braced the sides of his waist. "If I had wanted you to have that tape, I wouldn't have hid it in the shed."

"I have every right. You shouldn't have brought the damn thing into my house. And you tried to be sneaky about it." I adjusted the small bunch of string beans left on my lap. "In a gas tin. What's on the tape, Carl, what's so important that you'd go through so much trouble to hide it?"

He broke into laughter.

"You haven't watched it. Why is that, Elaine?"

"Whatever's on that tape I should find out from you, Carl. I'm your wife. I shouldn't have to go rummaging through a tool shed to figure out what's going on in your life. Just tell me the truth."

"You don't want to know." He backed up and leaned against

the sink. "If you really wanted to know you would have watched it already."

"What's on it, Carl? I deserve that much."

"Elaine—"

"Please."

"We're fucking—you happy now? Is that what you wanted to hear? We're having hot, butt-naked sex."

I jumped up from the table. Beans fell from my lap. When I walked down the hall and reached for the bathroom doorknob, Carl grabbed my dress from behind.

"Don't touch me," I said, pulling my dress from his grasp.

"Ellie, I'm sorry."

"Leave."

"Please, baby, let me explain."

"How could you do this to me? I love you . . . I love you, Carl."

"Don't cry, Ellie, please. I don't know. It's just—"

"It's just what?"

He stared at me, speechless. I hugged my arms and slid down the wall. Carl tried to pull me back up.

"Get away from me," I said. My chest heaved so hard I couldn't breathe.

"You shouldn't do this to yourself, Elaine. You need your inhaler?"

"Fuck you. You mothafucker." My voice went hoarse. "You did this to me. I didn't ask for this. You did this."

I sat at the bottom of the wall. The throbbing in my head made it hard to open my eyes. I slumped over and buried my face into my knees, my smock bunched around my stomach. Carl's footsteps blended with the ringing in my ears. He stooped next to me.

"Here," he said.

"Just go," I said into my knees.

"Don't hurt yourself because you're mad at me," he said. "Take the inhaler."

I slammed both hands into his chest and pushed him with all my strength. He barely budged.

"Damnit, Elaine. What's wrong with you?"

"I hate you. I hate you so much," I said, looking into his eyes.

"Come here."

He placed his hand on the back of my neck and pulled me into his chest. I hated him. Hated that I still loved the smell of Brut Musk permeating from his shirt fibers. Hated his arms strong around my back. He kissed my forehead, then my cheeks. His lips rested against my nose.

"Can a married man cheat on his mistress with his wife?" I said into his neck. His lips slid to mine. I felt his wetness melt into my mouth.

Chapter 7

June 9

He hasn't returned my phone calls. I left two messages on his office machine. Called back a couple of times just to hear his voice. I bet Glenda doesn't have this problem.

She kept thinking about eyes. Whatever was broken in her mother's had always been broken. It was just more noticeable now because brokenness ages in layers like skin. Caresses and tears sharpen from the inside out. She didn't want to be like M'Dea, but she was. Her eyes told her so. They shared the subtle nakedness of having been peeled.

Mingus flipped open the blue leopard print sketchbook. Slowly she ran her palm down the curve of her forehead. Her fingers opened over the width of her nose and closed on the ridges of her lips. She braced the blank page under her elbow and swept the pencil lead sideways down its length. In short overlapping strokes she re-created what her fingers had felt. She blended her cheekbones with her thumb and softened the folds of her eyelids with the rubbing motion of her index finger. Mingus stared at the page. The circling of ceiling fan blades tinted her likeness. She closed the book, careful to leave the shadows intact.

It was almost 6:30. Mingus swiveled her chair around and stared into the morning sky cut in half by the building's parking structure. She didn't mind the view; it motivated her. Two and a half more years before she'd be considered for partner. Selkirk, Higgins, Johansson, Mallory and Browning. Browning, Selkirk, Higgins, Johansson, and Mallory. Then she'd work toward equity partnership, she thought. Her father had always told her to go for it. Even harder than normal because she was a woman. A black woman. She'd done that. She had the second highest billable hour average in the firm. Her work was impeccable. She made sure of it with long hours and occasional full weekends and holidays. She liked law; sometimes she even loved it. But more often than not, she buried herself behind it because it held her together.

It was strange to her that she consistently worked in opposition to herself. What she used her career to forget, she often used visual art to remember. The silence had intrigued her from early on. The process of colors replacing words. She felt safer without sound. Like her hands were tied more closely to her spirit than her tongue. Growing up, she would sketch every night in the dining room. She'd spread out colored pens and pencils across the table-top, finish her homework quickly so she'd have the early evening to her imagination. The first thing she ever wanted to be was an artist. It was Eva who helped her to change her mind. Mingus remembered when they were kids how Eva used to sit with her girlfriends in the family room and tell them how she was going to be this bad-ass lawyer, how she was going to have a big office with two full-time secretaries working for her. On those days, Mingus would position her chair closest to the swinging doors and pretend she wasn't listening to their teenage declarations. Way back then, she decided that she wanted to be a lawyer too. Whatever a lawyer was.

6:45. Mingus read down her "things to do" list. *Schedule dropoff arrangements with Eva.* M'Dea had asked Mingus to drop off Eva's mail because Eva's car was on the blink again. Mingus checked her bag to make sure she'd remembered to bring it. Glancing at the rubber band-bound stack, she noticed an envelope with a printed state seal on top. The clear rectangular window displayed *Eva Chastity Browning*. It looked like a check. That's odd, Mingus thought. Eva didn't work for the state; she handled phone calls for a medical referral service. Mingus leafed through the rest of the envelopes. In the midst of junk mail and collection notices, she found an envelope with M'Dea's handwriting on it. She tore open a corner.

"Hey M'Dea, you up?" she said, holding the state check in her hand.

"Since five. I wanted to start seeding the winter vegetables and turning the soil before winter gets here."

"It's not even August."

Mingus squished the top and bottom of the envelope. The amount wasn't visible through the transparent window.

"Yeah, but it's going to be a cold one," M'Dea said, "I'm feeling it already. The stuff I'm doing will start sprouting soon anyway. Cabbage, onions, things like that. I don't want to be stuck planting in the dead of winter."

"Makes sense," Mingus mumbled. "How are you?"

"Just fine. Trying to make order of this house. It's amazing how much junk piles up over the years."

She wondered if M'Dea had started looking for financial records.

"Have you talked to Eva?" Mingus said.

"Not since Friday. She's pretty torn up about all of this."

Please, Mingus thought, Eva could brush off the Second Coming if she wanted to.

"Listen, M'Dea, why is Eva's unemployment check coming to your house and not to her apartment?"

"How did you know about that?"

"I have her mail. The check's on the top of the stack."

"You guessed, in other words."

"That's what lawyers do best. Why didn't you tell me she lost her job?"

"If she'd wanted you to know she would have told you, Mingus. You know how prideful she is; she was probably ashamed to tell you."

"Yeah," Mingus said, clicking her shoe on and off her heel, "ashamed to tell me she lost her job, but not too proud to take money from you."

"You shouldn't snoop. That's wrong, Mingus, and you know it."

"It's the only way to find anything out in this family. Everybody keeps a tight lip until stuff explodes." Mingus paused, contemplating whether or not to say the rest of what she was thinking. "And I still can't believe you weren't going to tell me—but you tell Eva of all people. I'm the one who can help you."

"And that's why I didn't tell you. You always have to come up with an answer. First thing out of your mouth was 'divorce him.' That's my decision, Mingus, and you can't make it for me. I talk to Eva because she listens—you decide you're going to be my lawyer."

"I'll drop off the mail tonight after work."

"Don't get defensive, baby. I love you, but I need to do this my own way."

"Fine."

"If you're going to be snippy, Mingus, I'm going to let you go." Mingus didn't respond.

"What time is your lunch break?"

"I'm not taking one today," Mingus said.

"Why?"

"Because I have a date tonight and I need to make up some time."

"I'll have Eva catch the bus over tomorrow."

"Fine. Just make sure she's here by one, please."

"She'll be there on time." M'Dea spoke softly. "And baby, don't let this situation with your father and me get you all worked up. We're adults, we can handle this. You worrying is not going to help anything. Just be happy, okay?"

"Too late."

"Try to have a good day, Mingus."

She'd come to the conclusion that her mother was a liar. She felt blasphemous for thinking it, but it was true. Why couldn't M'Dea just be honest? She wasn't fine and Mingus was tired of watching her pretend. It didn't shield Mingus from anything, it never had. It just made her heart hurt. Mingus was the only ten-year-old she knew who had a last will and testament. She didn't call it that, but from her favorite doll to her colored pencils, Mingus had bequeathed everything she owned to members of her family. Mainly Eva. There was something about the pain of being awake most of the night, lying in a dark room listening to muffled cries and arguments that the smiles at morning breakfast said didn't happen. One time she tried to talk to Eva about it and Eva told her she had made it all up. But children don't make up insomnia. Parents give it to them.

Mingus held down the intercom button.

"Have you finished the preliminary change of ownership reports?"

"I'm doing the last one now," Jolena responded.

"What about the Morrison notes?"

"I haven't transcribed them yet; I thought you wanted me to finish up the PCORs, then compile a list of assets for Sarah Davidson?"

"Send the Morrison notes over to central processing, please. I have a meeting at four and I'm going to need them."

"If you give me about ten minutes, I can do them myself."

"I can't wait. Make sure Monsha gets on them ASAP. If she's backed up, let me know."

"All right," Jolena said, "I'll take them over right now."

"Thanks."

Mingus pulled two red well folders from her briefcase. She opened the foundation file and flipped the worksheet to Article 3.12.6b. There was no way she was going to be able to finish all twenty-four sections by Friday unless she pulled fourteen-hour days. As she booted up her computer, Jolena knocked on the door.

"Come in."

"Here are the PCORs blue-backed and ready to go."

"Thanks. You can drop them in my in-basket."

Jolena tossed the paperwork in the top of four baskets and stood in front of Mingus's desk with her arms over her chest.

"What's wrong?" Jolena said.

Mingus didn't look up.

"Just busy."

"We're always busy. Give me the scoop."

"The scoop is," Mingus said recording a note to herself in her organizer, "that my billable hours were down last month and I need to increase my productivity."

"Mingus." Jolena shifted her weight onto her right leg. "It's June, you've already billed thirteen hundred hours. What are you trying to do?"

"Work, that's all."

"No, there's a problem. You even cut into me a few minutes ago. Whatever you think you're hiding, it's not working, Mingus. That much I know."

Mingus threw her head back onto the chair.

"Jolena, I would love to update with you right now. I hope you had a great weekend. I didn't. And right now my attention is on

51

finishing this foundation, my sister coming by on a lunch break I can't afford to take, and the two meetings I have this afternoon. Is that okay?"

Jolena shook her finger.

"I'm going to leave you alone for now. But when you want to talk about it, I'm not going to hold this against you."

Mingus waited until the door closed to allow the first tear to fall.

Chapter 8

I watched the tape. Must have been five o'clock in the morning. He thought I was asleep. I wasn't. I lay in a fetal position on my side, facing the back of his neck, staring at the mound his body made under the covers. It felt good to have him home again. My husband lying next to me in our bed. My arm draping his waist. Our feet touching. I wanted it to always feel like this. Like we fit again.

That's when he slid from under my arm, off the bed, into the shower. It occurred to me what was happening. I had become the other woman. It was my scent that had to be washed from his body. All I could do was lay there, helpless. Ask myself how I let it get to this.

He didn't turn on the lamp, just left the bathroom door agape to dimly light his way. He pulled fresh underwear and socks from the middle drawer. Fresh slacks and a white dress shirt from his side of the closet. He buttoned and zipped silently, careful not to wake me. Eyes barely open, I watched him through the slight flutter of lashes. It amazed me. How observable his process was. The ways in which I was covered up and washed away. I had witnessed firsthand my erasure. I wondered how many times I had been through this and not even known. My husband was preparing himself for another woman. The clean soap smell, the socks, none of it was for me.

I felt more like his mother than his wife. Like all of my milk had been given to groom him for the suckling of another's breast. I was silenced by the spectacle of my understanding. Carl was oblivious to me. He picked up his watch from the nightstand, slipped the gold band back over his wrist. Placed his wallet back into his right rear pocket. He was set. No goodbye. No kiss. Just picked up his shoes, clutched his car keys, and left.

I lay there, the wetness of our commingling plugged between my thighs, knowing that this would be the last of his semen to die inside of me. I absorbed the passing and let the balance dribble down my leg as I stood up. I had to watch the tape. I had to know what was so special about this woman that it made my husband leave my bed before sunrise. What did she have that I didn't?

I grabbed my robe off the bedpost. Tightened the pink draw-string around my waist. Tears started to roll, before I knelt beside the bed and pulled the black tape case from under the mattress. Before I walked barefoot down the hallway toward the living room. Before I sat on the couch with the remote in my lap. Before all of that, I knew I had lost.

I sat on the couch and tried to think about the old times. The times when we were good to each other. Like when we used to put the girls to sleep early just to pop popcorn and watch the Monday night movie. Like when Carl worked at Piggly Wiggly as a box boy and used to bring home peanut brittle every paycheck 'cause he knew I liked it. The times I used to change our bed-sheets midweek 'cause they'd be soaked in our sweat. There would be no more of these things between us. No more of the sweetness that held me over till next time.

The green light on the VCR blinked me back to reality. I took the remote in my right hand and pressed play. After a few seconds of black-and-white static, the blur gained focus. My heart solidified into heavy thumps. There she was. Sitting in some pale room, on a hunter green leather couch. The carpet was beige. The walls were beige.

Her skin was the color of maple syrup—not dark, like when it settles at the bottom of the jar, but golden brown like when it pours onto hot griddle cakes. Her blouse was a little darker than the walls. A low-cut cotton blend, tight, like Lycra was mixed in. A petite gold cross hung between her breasts. "Bitch," I said, not a tinge of hatred or disgust in my voice. "Black bitch."

I focused hard on her face until I felt nothing. Until every new quirk and twist was memorized behind my eyes. Then my gaze shifted back to the cross. The baby on her lap tried to grab it, but couldn't reach. I empowered the baby. Prayed her the strength to snatch the blasphemy from around the woman's neck. Her attention was won over by the rattle her mother shook in front of her. The child held the rattle awkwardly in one hand and angled it toward her mouth. That's when Carl's voice chimed in from behind the camera.

"Come on, Sarah. Say hi. Say hi, Sarah."

The woman shook her head at him.

"You know this chile can't say that."

"Both my girls started talking before eight months," he said. "At least Da-da."

"Well, give her space." The woman stood the baby up on her lap. "She'll talk in her own time. Won't you, honey? Yeah. Yeah, that's Mama's baby."

"Okay, scoot a little to the left so I can fit in the frame."

I stopped the tape. I didn't want to see his face. I didn't want to see his arm drape that woman's shoulder or know how her head rested sideways in the crook of his neck. But more so, I didn't want to look into his eyes and see how much he could forget me.

Chapter 9

June 11

We kissed for the first time. Steven held my face in his hand as he leaned across the table. He was soft and kind; I was horny.

His mother died in Marymont Hospital at 4:53 A.M. Steven was born at 3:20. He told Mingus this as they sat at the small round table sipping coffee after work. He felt like he knew his mother. He'd heard so many stories. Had photos of her at nineteen when she'd first met his father and used to ride on the back of his 1947 Harley FLH with the knucklehead engine. Her hair was dark and wild, he said. That's one of the things that attracted him to Mingus. Mingus was sure to tell him that on the day they'd met, she hadn't combed her hair that morning—just jumped up and went. All the better, he said.

She sipped iced coffee, mesmerized by the details he recalled of the mother he'd never met. Her long lashes. How her favorite stone was amethyst and she loved scrambled egg sandwiches with mayo on wheat. Mingus knew her own mother in much less detail. She didn't know what M'Dea's favorite food was. She knew she'd prepared pot roast and meatloaf with ketchup a lot when they were kids. That she hated dirty fingernails and put Vaseline on her feet at night then wore socks to bed.

She thought about what Steven had said at dinner. That a parent always loves one child more. Maybe he was right. That would explain the almost thirty years of disconnection she and M'Dea shared. The silences that appeared whenever just the two of them were in a room together. It was different with Eva. M'Dea always had something to talk to her about. One of them would disappear, then the other. They'd hole up in M'Dea's sewing room for hours. Dad and Mingus would be left on the couch. He'd pass Mingus the remote. They'd toss around conversation and laugh at the same punch lines on television. Mingus used to feel comfortable with that. But with her father gone, everything had changed. And she began to wonder if Eva had taken up all the intimate spaces missing from her experience with M'Dea. Or if maybe her mother had only enough trust for one daughter.

Every new emptiness she discovered inside herself made her desire for a child grow stronger. Later that night, as she lay in bed with paper-clipped pieces of the Devenol Foundation on both sides of her, she found herself rubbing the rise of her bare stomach. The bloating from her period had dissipated some, but the hard roundness was still there. Mingus sucked air in through her nose and watched her stomach bubble. She could have done it, she thought. Gotten pregnant. Not to trap him. But to have something in her life that stays.

During the end of their relationship, Keith had stopped lingering after sex. Immediately, he would pull out and jump into the shower. It was one, two, three—shower, kiss, leave. Mingus had started to see their relationship as more transactional than holy. A man entering her was sacred, but with Keith it had become methodical. A baby could have just been another part of the process. Sex, baby, shower, leave. She'd thought about it many times. But that wasn't her personality. She was the responsible type. The kind with an emergency account and always enough toilet tissue, lightbulbs, and AA batteries.

Mingus moved up from her stomach to her breasts. She cupped them tightly then let the brown-centered orbs shift to the sides of her ribs. The sag was delicate. Plums starting to lose the firm shine of deep purple. Fibers tearing away from one another with gentle pulling. Flesh growing soft. Skin letting go. The touch was better, she thought.

She left the light on this time. Slowly her fingers inched down-ward.

Chapter 10

Mingus was his first mistress. That's the irony of bringing female children into an unsettled relationship. A kind of competition occurs. Not just between sisters, but between all of the women in the household. When the favorite is chosen, it's like everyone knows that someone is walking around with a tiara between her ponytails.

I saw it the first time he held her. He hugged her five-pound swaddled body to his chest. He looked at her the way that I had always wanted him to look at me. Delicately. Completely present. It was almost like he had given birth to her himself. Or like she had birthed him.

So when Mingus asked me if I could sit back and accept another woman, the answer was yes. I had done it my whole life and made peace with it. Don't get me wrong, Glenda was a devastation. But a different kind. And that's what got me thinking about Sarah.

I remembered back to when we lived in his mama's house. After my father found out I was pregnant by a black man and chased me down the dirt road with his leather strap. I caught the bus to Alabama by myself the next day. Carl came four months later after his enlistment was over. We tried to get married right away, to give our child a proper birth and bring honor to Carl's family, but no one would marry us in Alabama.

For fourteen months we lived as husband and wife without a marriage certificate. Carl's mom, a petite woman everyone called M'Dea, told us we'd have to jump the broom and make do like many of her ancestors had done. So we did, that night in the living room. I dressed up in my eggshell white graduation dress. Carl wore some black trousers. And M'Dea held her kitchen broom stick as we jumped.

M'Dea and I grew close after that. She'd give me peppermint tea when I had morning sickness and I'd help her about the house and in the garden. One day, as we were drying dishes at the sink, I asked her if M'Dea was her middle name or her first. She squinted her eyes and said, "Chile, what kind of question is that? My middle name is Bernice. My first name is Orlene." That's when she explained to me that M'Dea was short for "my dear." I decided right then and there that that's what my children would call me.

M'Dea had an uncanny sense of knowing people. Sometimes I would stay in bed all morning under the pretense of not feeling well. She'd bring in a cup of Chamomile tea, sit it on the nightstand next to the Bible she'd placed in our room. Check my temperature with the back of her hand, then rub blessed virgin olive oil on my forehead and ripening belly. She'd tell me it was okay to miss my mom and pop. That they'd been the only two folks I'd known my entire life and that missing them was natural. I wouldn't have the strength to lie about it. I'd let the tears drip down the side of my face onto the pillowcase. She'd say, 'Chile, don't you mess up my pillows with that hard cryin', down is expensive nowadays.' We'd laugh. Then she'd take my face in her lap and let me cry some more.

She'd tell me everything would be okay after a while, that change just takes a little time. She'd say, 'And don't you worry yourself about that boy of mine. He's just like his daddy when he was young. Sleeping with his eyes open and his shoes on. He'll calm down after he gets some weight on his belly and some children under his belt."

Carl never calmed down. I got to thinking about how he used to sit out on the service porch every night humming Sarah Vaughan tunes. Playing them on his saxophone. Wishing he could travel and be a member of a band. Then I got to thinking about how Glenda's child had the same name.

I grabbed my knitting basket at my feet and placed it on my lap. Deep down, at the bottom, below my needle tray, was the envelope that held Glenda's business card.

Chapter 11

June 12

I couldn't sleep last night. Instead I sketched while I watched The Honeymooners and Father Knows Best on the oldies channel. No big revelations or anything, just found myself craving butterscotch and my parents arguing.

Mingus needed to apologize. Not for work's sake, but because of their friendship. They'd been working together since Mingus joined the firm almost five years prior. Jolena could practically read Mingus's mind and Mingus the same. That's why she knew Jolena was still mad at her—she was being far too nice and impartial.

Mingus ordered delivery for two and asked Jolena to join her for a lunch meeting.

"Hunan chicken with bok choy," Jolena said, *"unh hm."*

Mingus sat on one side of the desk. Jolena sat opposite her with crossed legs. Mingus watched her mix the food with a white plastic fork and take a bite. Before Jolena could finish chewing, she started talking.

"Somebody here needs to apologize to me so I can enjoy my food in peace."

She looked at Mingus.

"I'm sorry," Mingus said, "but you can talk enough crap to make a person—"

"Unh ah. Don't make you acting ugly my fault."

Jolena sat the Styrofoam container on her lap and took another bite. "What's wrong with you anyway?" she said.

Mingus closed her container of brown rice and mixed vegetables, then sat back in the chair.

"There's so much going on, I don't even know where to start."

"Pick a somewhere," Jolena said with a no-frills attitude.

"Before I say anything else, let it be on the record that you asked for this."

Jolena waved her hand.

"My father is cheating on my mother, she won't divorce him. I asked her to and told her I'd represent her. She said no—"

"Mingus, you're not a trial lawyer."

"I started out as a trial lawyer. And I'm not finished. To further the situation, my father will not return my phone calls, my sister lost her job, and I met a man."

"Well, at least the last part of that sounds promising."

Mingus smiled.

"He's white."

Jolena jumped up out of her seat.

"You are lying."

"No, really. Watch that sauce."

"You are lying through your teeth." Jolena wiped brown sauce off the outside of the container and placed it on Mingus's desk. "Since when do you date white men?"

"Since last Saturday and last night."

"Sookie, sookie now." She sat back down. "So do you like him; is this going somewhere, what?"

"It's only been two dates; it's too soon to tell. Only bad thing so far, besides him being a police officer, is that people paid so much attention to us. Staring. I found myself having to concentrate twice as hard just to block them out. Then this fine chocolate brother came up to me after our first date."

"Talking mess?"

Mingus rolled her eyes.

"Girl, yes. Talking about how I need to try loving a brother and getting loving from home."

"You know what that's about. He's talking about you getting loving from him."

"You know he is, he even slipped me his card."

"You gonna call him?"

"Jolena, no." Mingus covered her mouth.

"Why are you smiling then?"

"Can't a sister smile anymore?"

"Well, I'm just happy you have enough going on to keep your mind off of whatchamacallhim."

There was a knock on the door. Mingus figured it was Eva. She looked down at her watch. It was 1:20.

"Come in," she said.

Eva, wearing powder blue stirrup pants and thick-soled tennis shoes, walked over to the empty chair beside Jolena.

"Hey," Eva said. "Is this what y'all do all day?"

"You're late," Mingus said back. "Jolena, we can finish this up later this afternoon. Can you send out an FLP worksheet to Lossie Davis for me, please?"

"I'll do that right now. Hello, Eva," Jolena said passing her on the way out.

Mingus pulled the rubber band-bound stack from her bag and handed it to Eva.

"Here's your mail."

"What? You're not carrying a briefcase around like a big-shot attorney anymore?"

"I try not to mix business and personal items together, henceforth, briefcase—business, bag—personal."

Mingus swiveled away from Eva toward the credenza behind

her desk. She recorded the forty-five minutes she'd worked on the Morrison file.

"I never thought of you as the type who would give up power," Eva said, plopping down into the chair.

"Meaning?" Mingus said, still facing the computer. She could feel Eva staring at the back of her head.

"Cell phone, briefcase, plush suits. All your little power symbols. Some people need those things to feel important."

Mingus was still upset with Eva about the other morning. She felt the desire to lash out building in her stomach. She swiveled back around.

"Power is not what motivates me, Eva. And I don't have a cell phone."

"Let me clarify." Eva wagged her index finger at Mingus. "Most people think of power and money as the same thing."

"I'm not after money either, not in the way you're talking about."

Eva smirked. "What are you after then?"

Mingus coated her voice with a layer of faux calm.

"Why did you call me the other morning to tell me about M'Dea?"

"I thought you should know."

"At six A.M., Eva? Were you trying to get to me before Daddy did? Did you think M'Dea would call me herself?"

Eva flicked her hands in the air.

"I don't care what that man does and M'Dea wasn't going to tell you nothing anyway."

"How do you know that?"

"She even told me not to tell you, that's why."

Mingus shook her head.

"That's my point. It must have burned a hole in your tongue, huh? To know that Daddy screwed up and I didn't know about it. Was that it?"

"Fortunately"—Eva stood up and adjusted her blouse over the

waist of her pants—"I'm not one of your clients or lackeys. I don't have to tell you a damn thing. Thanks for the mail."

Mingus watched Eva exit as nonchalantly as she had entered. She was upset with herself for letting Eva get to her that way. She'd always gotten to her. Ever since they were kids. Used to be if Mingus did the slightest thing wrong, Eva would tattle her out shamelessly. Like when Mingus snuck a few sips of wine from the opened TJ Swan bottle in the refrigerator or when she started her period and hid the soiled sheet in a shoebox under her bed.

It was Mingus's biggest dream to get some dirt on Eva. When the two Richardson girls moved into the neighborhood, Mingus used to eavesdrop on the three of them as they talked about base-ment parties on the other side of town and which boys had the biggest ding-a-lings.

One time, Mingus knew she had Eva. It was getting dark and Mingus could see Eva inside the bathroom putting fade cream on her face. She'd gone with her and M'Dea to the drugstore the day they'd bought it. Eva had told M'Dea that she wanted the cream to lighten the dark skin around her elbows that made it look like she never took a bath. M'Dea agreed to buy it, but told her never to use it anywhere else on her body because it could ruin her skin. Catching sight of Eva in front of the bathroom mirror, Min-gus dropped her marbles at the edge of the grass and eased up be-hind a sweet gum tree about six feet from the window. She watched as Eva spread the thick white cream onto her neck, down her arms, and then recoated her face.

Mingus ran into the house, letting the screen door crash closed behind her. Hurriedly, she explained what Eva was doing and pulled M'Dea arm first toward the bathroom. M'Dea pushed open the unlocked door. She was caught. Instinctively, Eva rushed to M'Dea and hugged her tightly. Told her how the Richardson girls got all the attention from the boys because they were lighter-skinned like Mingus. The focus shifted. Instead of Eva getting punished for disobeying M'Dea, Mingus got sent to her room for the rest of the night.

Thinking about all this made Mingus crave something sweet. She pulled out the bottom drawer of her desk and reached into her purse. She recalled seeing three quarters in the change pouch. That would score at least a candy bar from the vending machine. Another thirty-five cents, and she could get a double-chocolate double-chip cupcake.

She unclasped the change pouch. Mixed in with the quarters and pennies was a crumpled business card: *Eric Simms, Special Programs Producer, WXBN Television.* Yeah right, she thought. Pompous ass. She mocked him aloud, "Try loving a brother, you might like it." If she hadn't tried anything else, she'd tried that. Mingus recrumpled the card and threw it in the wastebasket under her desk.

Chapter 12

I couldn't stop thinking about her. If I'd ever smelt her scent on his neck. If she cooked better than me or her breasts were firmer. Every time I tried to sleep, I saw her face tattooed behind my eyelids. Lipstick the color of hellfire on her lips. Cross hung around her neck.

One night, as I lay in bed, the television accompanying me into the wee morning, I wondered if she'd ever been here. I'd seen it on movies and talk shows, where the man brings the other woman to his house. Makes love to her in his marriage bed. I thought about the cruise Carl insisted I take to unwind. His *just because* gift to me. Four days didn't seem like a long time, Bahamas, midsummer, who could turn that down. I begged him to come with me. He insisted it was bad timing. The laundromat was just starting to gain a steady clientele. So I went by myself. I took in a few movies on the ship, ate lobster thermidor, read a romance novel.

Now I think about how my crystal salt shakers were in the spice cabinet instead of on the dining room table when I got back.

The bedsheets were changed and four steaks were missing from the deep freezer. I've never known Carl to want T-bones four nights in a row. But I dismissed all that. Came back feeling refreshed, wanting to work harder on our marriage.

I had to do something. She'd already taken my husband. I wasn't going to let her take everything.

Chapter 13

She dreamt about him. Her arms and legs spread-eagle, buttocks pressed tight against his unyielding mattress. He hovered above her like thick smoke. His sweat dripped into the dip between her shoulder and clavicle bone. Droplets slipped between her breasts. His arms outstretched. Her palms open. He didn't touch. Just pitched his body like a tent over hers and shared his heat.

Maybe she'd made a mistake. She could have at least called him. Given him a chance. She'd given Steven a chance. Look how that turned out. Her dad always told her to never put all her eggs in one basket. That was her modus operandus. She would stay until everything blew up and they both hated each other. Or at least until he found someone else and explained he needed some time to think.

Mingus sat at her desk flipping through notes from the Patterson meeting of the previous day. She needed to know. If the card was there—great. If the cleaning crew emptied it—at least there was the dream. Mingus closed her eyes and slid her hand under the desk into the wastebasket. Every other grab was a bunched-up piece of paper. "Yes," she said smiling, clutching the card between her fingers. Her hand twitched. She couldn't tell if it was excitement or fear. She decided to call before she lost her nerve.

"Reception desk."

"Yeah hello, may I speak to Eric Simms please?"

"One moment while I transfer you."

After a few rings another female voice picked up.

"Sorry, Eric's in the editing bay. Can I take a message and have him call you back?"

"Yeah sure, could you tell him Mingus Browning from Selkirk, Higgins, Johansson and Mallory called?"

"I'll give him your message."

Within seconds Mingus realized she hadn't left a number or anything for him to remember her by. He probably doesn't even recall my name, she thought. She picked up the receiver to call back but changed her mind. She didn't want to appear desperate. In the back of her mind, she wasn't sure if she should have called in the first place. She would wait. If the urge came back strong, she would analyze it. If it dissipated, she would let it go.

On her way back from lunch, she stopped at Jolena's desk to check for messages.

"I tried the new Ethiopian spot down the street. I brought back extra if you want to try it," Mingus said.

"I was just about to take a message. I saw you coming off the elevator and put him on hold."

"Patterson?"

"An Eric Simms."

"Oh my God," Mingus said.

"Sounds important. Who is it?"

"That's the guy," she whispered excitedly.

"The black one you weren't going to date?"

"Yes. Give me a second before you transfer him."

"Sookie, sookie now," Jolena said, rubbing one index finger on top of the other.

"Be quiet." Mingus ran into her office and sat on an edge of the desk. "Mingus Browning."

"Imagine my surprise hearing from you today."

"Are you sure you know whom you're speaking with?"

"Giovanni's. You drank a Shirley Temple."

"Cherry 7UP with a maraschino cherry. How did you know it was me?"

"I've only been living here a few weeks; a handful of people have my card. Besides, you don't meet too many people named Mingus."

"Oh," she said getting nervous again. "Well, this is a very busy week for me, I just came across your number in my Rolodex and wanted to touch base."

"I'm sorry to hear you're so busy. I was passed some phenomenal tickets to see *Ragtime* tonight. I would have loved for you to join me."

She pinched herself. "I could make an exception, even a busy woman needs R&R."

"Well, I don't know. I wouldn't want to throw you off schedule. It would weigh on my conscience if I was responsible for you losing momentum."

Does he want me to beg? she thought. She remembered how pompous and assuming he was at the restaurant.

"Are you always such an ass to people?"

"I don't know what you're talking about. And whew, such language coming from a lady. Are any of your coworkers in listening distance?"

He was calm and cool. Mingus hadn't ruffled a feather.

"No, no one is listening. I'm in *my* office, thank you, with *my* door closed and you know exactly what I'm talking about. You knew I wanted to go to dinner with you so you decided to be an ass. You probably weren't serious about asking me out in the first place. Just wanted to mess with me 'cause you saw me out with a white man."

"Do you always start conversations this way?" he said, mimicking what she had asked him at the restaurant. "Or is this your special way of letting me know I get to you and you don't know how to handle it?"

"You know what? I'm through with you. I don't want to go to dinner with you. I don't want to bear children with your non-mindreading ass, nothing. I don't want anything from you and the quicker you get that through your head, the better off you'll be. Don't call me again."

Mingus slipped the heel of her shoe back on her foot and paced back and forth in a straight line down the carpet. It occurred to her what bothered her most. He thinks he knows me, she thought. Thinks he can roll up in my life and set my world off balance. Like I've never had a real man before or something. She paced up and down a few more times shaking her hands, trying to relieve the tension in her arms and shoulders. I like Steven better anyway, she thought. He was challenging yet agreeable. And she was swamped with work. She didn't have time for a musical. She would work hard all week and see Steven Friday night as planned. She would forget about Eric Simms. Mingus promised herself.

After a while, Jolena walked in.

"Everything okay, Ms. Browning?"

"Everything's fine," she said and tapped her fingers on the desk. "And where'd that 'Ms. Browning' come from? Please. You better go play secretary somewhere else. I have a problem with you anyway. Ever since you got that boyfriend, you ain't got time for a sister."

Jolena put both hands on her hips.

"This is not about me. Just tell me what happened."

"This damn man. I don't understand. Every time we talk he ends up getting on my last nerve."

"That bad?"

"Yes," Mingus said.

"Can you talk it out?"

"Hell no. We can't even have a decent conversation. In all the time you've known me, how often have you heard me curse?"

"Two, three times."

"See, that's what I'm talking about. He makes me lose it. I get to talking to him or thinking about him, and I end up going somewhere I don't need to go."

"Sounds like love to me."

"Ms. Jordan, don't you have some work to do?"

"I'm free; my boss is doing enough work for the two of us." Jolena laughed. "Really though, Mingus, it sounds like he gets to you and that can't be all bad. Give him a chance."

"Are you finished?"

"No. Let's go to the movies tonight."

"To see what?" Mingus said, crossing her arms.

"Whatever."

"I'm not feeling it today."

"See, you're still thinking about him."

Mingus rolled her eyes.

"You can roll your eyes all you want, but I'm not letting you off that easy. You were just complaining that I don't spend time with you anymore. Let's at least go to dinner—we both have to eat. Right after work?"

"If we can both get out of here by six, I'll go."

"See you at six."

A few minutes before six, Mingus heard a tap on the door.

"Give me one second," she yelled, gathering some papers she was taking home.

The footsteps were soft.

"These are for you."

A deep voice hovered over her desk. She looked up.

"Eric," she said.

"I hope you like wildflowers," he said, looking like the poster boy for Conroy's, holding a bouquet of exotic flowers in his hand. "They reminded me of you."

"What are you doing here?" She hid her joy behind a hard tone.

"I wanted to apologize. I didn't mean to get on your bad side."

"I thought I told you I didn't want to see you again?"

"You told me a lot of things, but you haven't told me if you accept my apology."

She looked at him, extending his hand across the desk, looking scrumptious in a black double-breasted suit that was buttoned. His waist was svelte.

Mingus stood up. Shook his hand with one hand and reached for the flowers with the other.

"I'll take these," she said.

"Will you have dinner with me tonight?"

"Can't. I have plans." She wanted to smile.

"You move quick."

"Sometimes it happens like that."

"Tell me something," he said, "if you didn't have plans, would you have had dinner with me?"

"What difference does it make?"

"Maybe I'm sentimental."

"Maybe." Mingus smirked.

"That looks like a yes."

"You should know; you're the mind reader."

Mingus attempted to slip her hand from his but Eric held on.

"What if I asked you to cancel?"

"We both know you ain't got it like that."

"Will you cancel?" he said sweetly, massaging her hand with both of his.

"Hell no." Mingus pulled her hand away. She was happy to get him back for not asking her when he had the chance. "And actually, you should be going. Thank you very much for the flowers."

"Is your date meeting you here?"

"Yes."

"What if I kept you company until he got here?"

"Look—"

"No ulterior motive. I just want to share a moment with you."

"Why?"

"Find out a little about you."

"Like what?" She folded her arms over her chest.

He slid his right hand into his pants pocket and braced his chin with the other.

"Like, if it's serious between you and the man I saw you with at the restaurant."

"I like to keep my personal business private."

"Maybe I'd like to become your personal business."

His expression was serious. Mingus sucked in air between her teeth and tried to shake the chill he'd sent down her spine.

He stared her in the eye and four feet from those soft brown lips was too close for Mingus.

"How do you know you want that?" she said, shifting her focus between his lips and his eyes.

"Maybe it's the way your lip quivers when we talk, or the way you suck air through your teeth and think I don't notice, or maybe it's my spirit man telling me you're the woman I need."

"It's time for you to go."

She snapped closed her briefcase and turned to straighten some folders on the credenza. She needed to catch her breath.

"Looks like your date is late."

Mingus looked down at her watch.

"Did I tell you what time they were coming?"

"Maybe I already knew."

"And how would you know that, Mr. Simms?" she said, facing the window, breathing slow through her nose.

"Maybe because I'm the date you're waiting for. What would you say to that?"

"I'd say you're about a foot too tall and you have a penis."

"And what if I told you I spoke to your previous date earlier and she suggested I get here a little before six to give her time to slip out of the building?"

"I'd say you set me up."

"More or less."

"Why didn't you tell me this from the beginning?"

"I wanted to surprise you. Feel you out. See if you were still interested or if you really wanted me to leave you alone."

Mingus removed her suit jacket from the back of her chair and pulled it over her arms. "Did you get your answer?"

"The play starts at eight. Would you like to accompany me?"

"We'll take my car."

Chapter 14

Filing for divorce is like your last day of high school and knowing you're never going to see any of your friends ever again. But I'd already been through that and this was much worse. Two weeks after I graduated high school I ran away with Carl. Bought a dollar-fifty plastic bouquet from Kroftman's thrift and used my eggshell white, off-the-shoulder graduation outfit for my wedding dress. Wasn't much hope in me trying to stick around Wilmington. No doubt my father would have killed me; the way he ran me out of the house showed me that. Felt like a pack of beer-guzzling wolves on my heels. All I could do was hold my stomach and run. Protect my baby and run. To this day, my only real regret was never saying goodbye to my mama.

Losing Carl is indescribable. How do you lose the one thing you've lived your life for? It's like all these years he's been my only living relative, my only connection to an identity, and now I have to pull the plug. A part of me wonders if I should just keep the connection to feel safe. But deep down, underneath all of the anger and disappointment, I ask myself, What would I be living for without him? Only answer I come up with is—I don't know.

Chapter 15

June 15

I found a gray hair in my pubic area last week. One shining silver strand in a sea of black. I don't even have any gray hairs on my head yet. Makes me wonder if it means something.

Mingus got into work early the next morning and waited for Jolena to arrive. She was working on the Devenol Foundation when she heard Jolena's computer boot up. Mingus pressed the intercom button, "Ms. Jordan, this is Mingus J. Browning."

"Yes, what can I do for you?"

"May I see you, please?"

"Right away, Ms. Browning."

Jolena walked into the office with a steno pad in hand and closed the door behind her.

"You may have a seat."

"Thank you, Ms. Browning."

"Now, what the hell were you thinking?"

Jolena started to laugh. Mingus broke her serious expression with a smile.

"Don't be mad at me, Janay," Jolena said. "He sounded so sweet and sincere."

"Um humph. Don't try to get back in by using my middle name—you sold me out."

"Stop, no I didn't."

"Yes you did, and you know it."

Jolena leaned forward resting her elbows on Mingus's desk. "Who was sitting in here pouting because she didn't think she was going to hear from him again?"

"Purely circumstantial. Is that the best you can do?"

"Answer me this, did you have a good time?"

"I plead the fifth," Mingus said.

"Was he good company?"

"The fifth."

"Do you feel you enjoyed yourself more with him than you would have going to dinner with me?"

"Definitely yes." Mingus took a quick sip of coffee. "What I want to know is how he got you to help him."

"First he introduced himself and explained that he had ticked you off and wanted to make it up to you, then he asked if I would help him."

"Oh, and being the close and dedicated friend that you are, you said, 'No, I could never betray the trust of my good friend Mingus by lying and scheming.' "

Jolena smoothed her fingers through her straight black hair.

"No. I said, 'Of course I'll help, what do you need me to do?' Then we set it up."

"Set *me* up, you mean."

"It, you, whatever. It all served the same purpose. You like him, huh?"

She didn't answer. Just rubbed her hands on the outside of the mug.

"Yeah, you like him."

"I can't even help it. He said something to me that blew my mind."

"What?"

"That he wanted to be the main part of my private life and that he doesn't want any company."

"What?" She put her hands on her hips. "And you've known him how long?"

"Not even a week."

"You better be careful," she said, pointing her index finger. "I did notice a slight accent, he might be one of those undercover African brothers trying to take back an American wife to add to his collection."

"He's from Chicago. And moving a little fast can work sometimes."

"Those are your hormones talking. You know where that's going to lead."

Mingus rolled her eyes and grabbed her coffee.

"We just had a good time, that's all."

"Yeah right. Next date he'll be trying to hit the skivvies."

"When did you become clairvoyant?" Mingus said.

"You don't have to listen to me, but you know I'm right."

"Not on the second date. He won't try anything."

"When did *you* become clairvoyant?" Jolena smirked.

Mingus bit her lip to keep in the laughter.

"You can't even stop giggling. I'm serious, Mingus, you sound like you thinking about giving it up."

Mingus gave her a blank stare and leaned back in the chair.

"You nasty heffa," Jolena said.

"Like you should talk. You have built-in penis at home. Hittin' it like a glass of water. Eight ounces, eight times a day."

"Don't blame your scandalousness on me." Jolena crossed her arms over her chest.

"How long did you and Mikhail wait before you did it?" Mingus stared her in the eye and clicked her nails on the desktop while waiting for an answer.

"I plead the fifth," Jolena said.

"I thought so. You forget I *knew* you when you first met the Negro."

"Handle your business."

Mingus's apartment was upstairs facing an open field of thick grass and wildflowers. Sometimes, when she left the front windows open, she could smell whiffs of jasmine and rosemary scenting the air. She dropped her shoes and briefcase next to the planter beside the door and unbuttoned the first six buttons of her green acetate skirt. I must be gaining weight, she thought. I used to be able to get this skirt down over my hips in four buttons.

Mingus laid her skirt and jacket on the couch and walked over to the oak entertainment center against the far wall. She flipped through radio personalities and soulful grooves until she chanced upon some jazz, bluesy and mellow like what was playing when she first saw Eric. All she needed now was a nice round cup of Merlot. She pulled the bottle of wine from the portable wine rack in the kitchen, poured half of a glass, and walked back into the living room toward the answering machine on her desk. The display flashed two messages. Steven and Eric, she thought. She was right; the first message was from Steven, just thinking about her, looking forward to seeing her Friday night. The other message was from Keith. She glanced at the dried-up rose on her desk.

Keith. The man who jumped up in the middle of their seemingly going somewhere ten-month relationship and decided to move out of state.

Mingus, hey. I haven't heard from you since I moved back to the city. I left my new number on your machine a few weeks ago. Let me make sure you have it, 212-555-4766. Again, 212-555-4766. Call me when you get a chance. I'd like to talk to you. Peace.

Run away from me then try to pull me back in from five states away? Yeah right, Mingus thought. She left the empty wineglass on her desk and made her way to the bedroom. She still missed him, but she wasn't going to let him throw a wrench in her program. Eric would be picking her up in less than an hour.

Mingus bent down and pulled a pair of black sweats and a B.U.M. sweatshirt from the base drawer of the dresser. She opened her underwear drawer. She was torn between a black lace G-string and red French-cut silk. She rolled down her pantyhose to her ankles and let the granny panties she was wearing hang around her knees. She checked the panty liner in the center of the crotch. No blood. She bent her knees and slowly eased her middle finger into her vagina. The walls were clear, only a pale trace of color was left.

Can't a woman just escape for a while? she thought, slipping her legs into the black thong. She'd waited five months before having sex with Keith and look where that got her. Maybe Eric would be different. And maybe if she stopped trying to be perfect, she could just be human.

Mingus pulled off the vanilla silk chemise and clasped a black lace bra between her breasts. She looked at herself in the scalloped mirror attached to her dresser top. Her stomach was still slightly pouched from her period. Mingus turned around and checked out her backside. She'd always had hips and an ass, and looking in the mirror, she'd finally come to the conclusion that neither were going anywhere.

She sat down on the couch with a crossword puzzle from the Sunday paper. Eric would be arriving soon and she was losing conviction. Was she using him? She didn't like the sound of that; she'd never just slept with someone for sex sake. She liked Eric, but like Jolena said, she really didn't know him. And then there was Steven. Talking to him every night after his shift. She had his home, pager, cell and work numbers. Mingus liked him too. She liked the way he'd held her face when he'd kissed her. He was almost the perfect guy—strong, attentive, funny. Maybe if she'd been more open she could have seen him that way. She didn't. She couldn't never stop thinking that he was white and she was black, no matter what her genetics said.

The doorbell rang, accompanied by two knocks. Mingus walked to the door.

"You're early," she said.

"Yeah, we wrapped up sooner than I expected."

"Come in."

Eric wiped his boots on the doormat. "I love all the plants you have around the place," he said, as he followed her over to the couch.

"I got my green thumb from M'Dea—I mean my mom."

Her palms were starting to sweat. Mingus tucked her hands under her thighs.

"That's what we used to call my grandmother," Eric said. "Listen, would you be terribly disappointed if I took a raincheck for tonight?"

"Damn, ditching me already?" Eric nudged Mingus's hand from under her leg and held it in his. "Was it the bowling or the pizza that got you?"

"Neither. It's just, I'm feeling kinda funky this evening."

"Anything I can do?"

Eric leaned toward her, caressing her hand with the tips of his fingers. Mingus drew her hand back into her lap.

"I think I'm just going to take a bath and relax."

"You sure?"

"Yeah," Mingus nodded, staring directly at his lips, smelling the vanilla balm that slicked them.

"You wouldn't deny a man a consolation hug, would you?"

Eric stood up and pulled Mingus by both hands to her feet. The top of her head reached just below his clavicle bone.

"You look beautiful," Eric said, lips barely moving.

Mingus looked up into his eyes.

"That must be a mack line. My sweats are barely black anymore."

"I'm talking about the woman, not what you have on."

He moved in closer. She could feel body heat radiating from his sweatshirt onto her face. He scooped his arms under hers and pressed his open palms gently into the center of her upper back, pulling her closer to him. She let out a jagged breath on his chest. He cocked his head slightly and kissed the right side of her forehead.

"Your back is tense," he said, breath smooth against her skin.

"Yeah, it's been that kind of week."

"You know, I made my way through college as a masseur."

"Sure you did," Mingus said, letting her face rest on his chest.

"Only one way to find out."

He kneaded his fingers under her shoulder blades up to the base of her neck. His hands traveled her body like he knew her. Mingus's head slumped into his chest. She remembered the dream—him tongue-tying her with each touch, her breathing in his heat through her nose.

"You gotta go," she said.

Eric spoke into the wildness of her hair. His breath tingled onto her scalp.

"That's the second time you've told me that. I figure it's about thirty minutes to my place from here. I could set up my table, pull out the Emu oil."

"Nuh, uh."

"You're already dressed; we could leave right now."

"Why're you trying to break me down?" Mingus asked with her eyes.

"You don't have to let me," Eric replied back.

Eric parked in front of a cabin-style house with rustic wood shingles and palm-size rocks built into the lower three feet of the front wall. Mingus glanced at him as he unfastened his seat belt. He wore loose blue jeans and a slightly oversize sweatshirt. The house reminded her of him—comfortable and masculine.

They entered around the side through the kitchen. Silver pots with copper bottoms hung over an island in the center of the room. Bright white tile with yellow trim covered the countertops. The stove was shining silver with no food on top, but Mingus could smell the remnants of spiced food—maybe Creole, maybe Indian, she thought. She walked over to the sink. An empty vegetable hanger hung above it. The fixtures were spotless, like either he never cooked or was a complete neat freak.

"Like a quick tour?" Eric said.

"Sure."

Mingus followed him through an arched hallway into the living room. The floor was the color of sliced almonds, almost white wood, with a thick layer of gloss covering the surface. A waist-high, carved African warrior statue stood in front of two wood-framed glass doors that opened inward. The rest of the room was empty except for a black phone with a coiled cord sitting in the corner.

"I haven't decided what to do with it yet."

"The floors are great. Where does this go?" Mingus pointed to a staircase that descended from the deck, separating it into two halves.

"To the beach. There's a dock under the deck for porting a boat. I'm not really thinking about buying one. I'm an ocean-fishing man myself."

Mingus smiled.

Down the main hall on the right was a guest bedroom with an adjoining bathroom. On the left, a weight room with padded floors and another room Eric called his getaway room.

"You need all this to relax, huh?" Mingus said, still holding his hand. The door opened to a wall-to-wall stereo system and plush burgundy chairs arranged in a half-moon facing a large screen built into the wall.

"Yep, music and old movies on a big screen with a bag of white cheddar popcorn."

"I thought you've only been here for three weeks?" She pulled his hand.

"I had it done before I got here. I wanted to move in and feel at home. We better get started. You can change in the bathroom down the hall. I have a massage table in the weight room."

Mingus gave him a look. She couldn't figure out if he was pimp of the year or the man of her dreams.

"Change into what?" she asked.

"There's a terry cloth robe hanging in the bathroom; you can change into that." He rolled both his wrists. "I'll be in the weight room setting up."

Mingus headed across the hall to the bathroom. She immediately heard a knock on the door.

"Yeah," she said through the door.

"You can take off your socks and put on my slippers."

"Thanks." She hoped he wasn't one of those men with athlete's foot; she'd been through that already.

She walked up on him from behind, wearing the black terry cloth robe and leather slippers. He had turned the heater on and the warmth coated her face and legs.

"On the table," he smiled, glancing back at her.

Mingus faced the table and untied the robe slowly. Laying face down, she couldn't see Eric but she could hear him rubbing the oil briskly between his hands. When he touched her the first time, her body went into shock. Warm, oily hands enveloped her shoulders. She could feel all his fingers kneading into her flesh.

"Your shoulders are tight," he said, concentrating on a knot in her right shoulder.

"I think that's where I store tension."

"Try stretching a few times a week."

"Yeah," Mingus said, paying more attention to his hands than his words. "Right there."

"This is tense too," he said, massaging her lumbar region. "You should probably get a massage once a week, at least till the bugs are worked out. Your muscles need to get used to being relaxed."

"I agree," she mumbled to him, while thinking to herself she'd lucked up. Lord, please let this man be who I think he is, she prayed.

His fingers journeyed down her lower back to her behind. Her gluts rolled like dough under his fingers.

"Try not to tense up," he said.

His hands worked her thighs and down to the soles of her feet. "Okay, turn over."

She turned onto her back and noticed that her nipples were hard. She looked at him to see if he noticed, but his expression was business as usual.

"Would you like a towel to cover your chest until I get to it?"

"No," Mingus said.

He pushed his fingers into the spaces between her toes and wiggled them into submission. After massaging her calves, she watched him squeeze more Emu oil into his hands. He pressed her lower thigh. Chills ran through her body. His fingers inched upward, parting her legs a little with each movement. Her breaths got short and heavy as he kneaded the inner flesh. She braced her hands on either side of the table and tried not to squirm. Eric rolled the lace panties an inch into her hairline. Mingus closed her eyes. With four fingers he massaged her pelvic muscles. Her bottom lip quivered. She held her breath. Eric moved up both sides of her stomach to the outside of her breasts. In small circular motions his fingers moved inward toward her nipples until they swelled with color in his hands.

"Ahh." Mingus's body started to squirm. "Eric, ahh."

His hands plunged deeper into her breast.

"Please," she said.

His fingers moved to her neck. Her body twisted and turned like a thousand kneading hands swarming her body.

He stood above her head and leaned in close.

"The neck should never be handled roughly," he said.

Mingus watched the sexy groove of his lips as he talked—how his tongue slid across pink-purple flesh leaving a trail of moistness behind.

Eric finished her neck with feather soft caresses and took Mingus's hand. She followed him upstairs, past two closed doors into his bedroom. The carpet rose and fell under her feet. Eric let go of her hand and bent down a few feet in front of her, lighting the fireplace with a long wooden match. Mingus stood still, watching the movement of the flame. Still on his knees, he pulled his sweatshirt over his head. The orange shadows hugged his curly-haired chest. Shit, Mingus thought. He pulled her into him like he had in her living room. They stood on their knees, bare chests touching.

Bending her head into his lap, he slid his open palm down her back. The roll of her skin between his fingers caused a rippling under the surface, each wave more intense than the one before. Eric held the back of her neck in his left hand and with his right, pulled two pins from her hair. "It's over," Mingus said into his lap, all resistance gone from her body. He massaged her scalp with strong hands. His skin met the fire at her roots. He was burrowing into a private place. A place where the right man's comforts could sooth away distrust and bad endings. A place where she loved like the first time. A place where she wanted to be touched.

"Eric," she gasped, shaking her head.

"Relax, baby."

All she could do was breathe.

He laid her on her back and looked down at her as he unbuttoned his jeans. The first button popped from its slit. His legs were thick; his ass a sprinter's—firm, wide, tight, and black.

"I can't take this."

No response. No smile. He stared her in the eye like he was meaning business. Kneeling between her ankles, he raised her foot to his mouth. He licked up her calf and bit the tendon above her heel. Mingus grabbed for his chest. He dodged his bald head into her pubic hair and careened it about until her legs spread into eagle wings and she was holding his ears, pumping to his rhythm. Mothafucka. Mingus vowed right then and there—only a bald man belonged between her legs.

Mingus's back tensed into an arch, her fingers suctioned to the back of his head. He snatched her hands away and stretched them high above her head, holding her crisscrossed wrists with one hand. With the other, he reached under the bed. His body covered her like a second skin. He placed a black-and-gold square between his teeth and ripped it open. Mingus closed her eyes. Anticipation caused her to gyrate as his hip forced her legs to open wider. She had never been so wet. As he worked into his groove, he placed his hands in hers and began to rise and fall on top of her like a heavy blanket making smoke signals over fire.

He rode faster and faster, then slowed his entire body to a halt except for his penis that pulsed small vibrations through her tightening pelvis.

"I can't take this," she said shutting her eyes, "it's too much."

Eric grabbed the sides of her face almost gently.

"Look at me. You can take this. Let your body relax. Trust me. I got you."

Mingus softened her apprehensions and let her body be enveloped.

"Right there, baby?"

"Yes," she whispered into his neck.

"Work it, Ming. Yeah, you got it baby. Awh yeah." He rode faster and faster. "You gonna make me come. Work it, Ming."

Ming. She hadn't been called that in a long time. Her dad used to call her that when she was little. Eva used to tease her about it, "Daddy's Ming," she would say with contention in her eyes.

Eric kissed her stomach and rolled onto the rug. He nudged her onto his chest. She maneuvered her head under his chin. He smoothed her hair out of his face.

"You want to go home tonight?" he said.

"No."

Eric hugged her tighter. "Did you come?"

"Yeah, what about you?"

"You know I did. You were working and wiggling."

Eric gyrated, pretending to be her.

"Be quiet. You tried to work me to death."

"Bed is no place to be holding back."

"I'll remember that next time."

She raised her head off his chest and smiled. Firelight flickered in his eyes.

"If you got more I'll take it," he said.

"You're smooth, aren't you?"

"What are you talking about?"

He wrapped his arms around her back and kissed her nose.

"I can't explain it, but I feel it. Like, why did you call me Ming?"

He craned his neck up to look at her.

"I called you Ming because that's how I think of you. My Ming."

"Don't you think that's kind of soon?"

"What is is. Not everything has a formula."

"You're too much." Mingus smiled and rolled back onto the rug.

"That doesn't mean you're going to leave here and go back to the white boy, does it?" he asked.

Jenoyne Adams

"Now what are you talking about?"

"The guy you were with at the restaurant."

"Steven?" She furrowed her eyebrows. "That was our first date."

"Your first and last?"

"Are you marking territory?" Mingus said, fighting the urge to put her hand on her hip. "I haven't even started to get in your closet—like how many women you left back in Chicago, how many you've met and slept with since you've been here. You're not exactly on the table."

"Two."

"Two what?" Her heart slipped into her stomach.

"I've slept with two women since I've been here. One I met at an industry party my first few nights in town and you."

Mingus glanced at the palm-size condom box at the edge of the bed. There was one condom left. All at once she felt cold inside.

"Can I have some cover?" she said, turning on her side.

Eric pulled the paisley comforter off the bed.

"I hope I didn't make you uncomfortable. It wasn't anything."

"What wasn't anything?" She could feel angry tears collecting behind her eyes. You did this to yourself, Mingus, she thought.

"The girl," Eric said sitting up, his palms resting on his bent knees, "it was nothing. I had just gotten in town, we laughed, had a few jokes and then—"

"Yeah, then you brought her back to your place for a massage and fuck in front of the damn fireplace."

"No. She was a flight attendant only in town for the weekend and we went back to her hotel. When I said you were the only person I've brought to my place I meant it."

"Whatever, Eric." Mingus burrowed her face into the comforter.

"Don't 'whatever' me, Ming." He reached down and turned her face toward him. "I met you while you were on a date with another man. He was staring you up and down and you were returning the energy. Today, I get to your place, you tell me you're having a horrible day after we had a wonderful date last night. All I can figure is that you're having problems with your man."

"I was having family problems. My father is—I wasn't lying to you."

"Your father is what, Mingus?" He spoke delicately, but firm.

Mingus looked him in the eye and shook her head.

"Cheating on my mother."

"Damn. That's a lot," Eric said.

Mingus turned on her back and stared at the ceiling.

"I don't know what's going to happen. My mother has never worked outside the home a day in her life, she has no resumé, no true way to make an income. She won't let me handle her case. I haven't talked to my dad in months. He's not returning my phone calls. Only thing that's somewhat normal is my relationship with my sister, Eva, and that's because we don't have one."

"Sibling rivalry?"

"It passed the sibling rivalry stage a long time ago." Mingus folded her arms over her eyes. "She just lost her job. I know she's going to be needing rent money, not to mention groceries. Unemployment isn't going to cover everything. But she's too damn proud to ask me for anything."

"What if you helped her get a job?"

"There are some openings at my office, but I don't think that would work." Mingus took a deep breath. "See what happens when you open up a can of worms, Eric?"

"What kind of skills does she have?" he said, ignoring her comment.

"Basic computer, good verbal skills, typing. I don't know what's all on her resumé, but the girl's not stupid by any means."

"Listen," Eric said, resting on one elbow, facing Mingus, "the woman who's currently my assistant got promoted to research coordinator; maybe I could interview your sister."

"Are you serious?" Mingus took her arms from over her eyes.

"I can't promise anything, but I'll talk to her."

"You'd do that for me?"

Eric leaned in, kissing her lips then forehead.

"Your sister's gonna be fine; your family's gonna be fine. You just have to believe that."

Mingus shook her hands. "This is not real," she said.

"What?"

"This whole thing. It's like you rode into my life on a white horse, and I stopped believing in white horses a long time ago."

Eric didn't cut her any slack. "Maybe that's why you're by yourself."

Mingus flipped the blanket off of her and attempted to get up. Eric grabbed her and pulled her to him.

"I'm not any of those men you've been with, Mingus. I'm not a dog; I'm not a saint either, but I'm not a dog. And sometimes you women say you want a good man in your lives but you're not willing to do the healing it takes to have one."

"What, you think I'm bitter or something?" Mingus said.

"Those are your words, and let's get off this topic before we have our third argument."

She was scared, and he was making too much sense. Mingus lay on his chest and pretended to fall asleep.

When she woke up the next morning, she didn't see Eric. 6:03. She grabbed his sweatshirt off the chair next to the bed and put it on. Approaching the stairwell, she could hear two voices. He was talking to a woman. The flight attendant popped into her head. Mingus pulled the sweatshirt over her pantyless crotch and walked to the bottom of the stairs. The smell of cooked bacon flowed from the kitchen. She peeped around the corner.

"Hey baby, come on in. This is Guillermina." He motioned toward a young woman with black hair flowing down her back. "She keeps the house and makes sure I'm fed well." Eric sipped his juice and looked up at Guillermina. "This is my girl, Mingus."

"Good to meet you," Guillermina said with a thick Spanish accent, and a stiff smile.

"Morning," Mingus said, stretching her arms behind her back. The young woman looked about twenty-three and had on a pair of black pedal pushers with a tight sleeveless red sweater showcasing her perky little breasts. Bet she can't bend to get Dutch cleanser from under the sink, Mingus thought.

"She's almost finished with breakfast," Eric said. "You hungry?"

Mingus wasn't eating anything she had cooked.

"I have a client meeting at nine. I need to get home to get changed."

"I was hoping we'd have time for a quick breakfast."

"How about I cook you breakfast in the morning at my place."

Guillermina turned from the stove and stared at Eric.

"Sounds good," he said, smiling back at Mingus.

"I'm gonna go get changed."

Mingus walked back down the hall, past the staircase to the bathroom. She got that sinking feeling again. Like the emptiness she felt when her period came. The same feeling she felt when she broke up with someone or looked into Eva's eyes. What if she lost Eric too? She slipped her legs into her sweats and left his sweatshirt on.

They were giggling when Mingus walked back into the kitchen. Guillermina held a half-eaten slice of bacon between her fingers. Mingus bit her lip.

"You ready?" Eric said.

Mingus nodded. Eric stood up and wiped syrup from his lips.

"Mina, I'm out of here. If you could leave a pasta in the fridge for dinner I'd appreciate it."

"Chicken pasta with zucchini and yellow peppers?"

"Perfect." Eric drank the last of his orange juice. "I won't be here tomorrow morning so I'll see you Thursday."

Mingus stared out of the passenger window. She didn't notice the trees or parents packing their children up for school. She didn't notice the morning joggers or brisk walkers with sticks in their hands. She thought about his words. *Mina. Ming.* Was this his way of getting close to women. Shortening their names to make them feel like he understood something special about them. *Ming.* She did feel special when he called her that. Maybe she was just being foolish. Trying to fall too fast—again. You should have waited, she told herself. What if he was the one? She wanted to tell him that she hadn't done a one-night stand since college—undergrad. That she really was the kind of girl a man could settle down with. Eric made a right onto the freeway on-ramp. A deflated tear trickled between her lips.

"Thinking about something?" Eric said, nudging her shoulder.

Mingus licked the salt from her lips.

"My family," she said.

"You're going to give your sister my number, right?"

"Yeah, of course."

"You can't worry yourself."

Eric flashed a quick smile. Mingus grinned. She wanted to close her eyes tight and wrap herself up in him. He made her feel safe. Mingus turned her body toward Eric.

"I was thinking," she said, "maybe we could do dinner tonight at my place."

"I kinda like the sound of that—dinner, Mingus, breakfast, Mingus."

Dinner, Mingus, breakfast, Mingus? "I hope you're not getting the wrong idea, Eric." Her voice rose an octave. "I'm not easy, despite how this looks."

"Are you saying I'm special?"

Mingus folded her arms around her waist.

"I'm saying I don't want you to misconstrue my intentions."

Eric glanced at Mingus and merged into the far right lane.

"Let me be real with you, okay? If I thought you were a *ho,* I would have taken you to a hotel, not to my house. So relax, all right?"

Mingus smiled and turned back toward the window. She pretended to relax, but inside she was still spinning.

Chapter 16

I carried them in a box. A Christmas box, the kind you wrap a nice-size book in or a thick knit hat and scarf. I placed them in one by one. The lipstick and pearl earring, her business card, six credit card statements showing movie, concert, and lingerie purchases. Next were three letters, arranged in order of which hurt me worse. Then the birthday card, Christmas card, and Valentine's Day card. Then the videotape in a black plastic case. I put what I could find of our bank records and other financial documents in a manila envelope.

The lawyer barely looked in the box. Said we live in a no-fault state, so proving fidelity or infidelity wasn't important to my case. Said that after thirty-five years, since everything we own is community property, I would basically get half. More than half if substantial spousal support needs could be established.

How do you take away the emotions and commitments of marriage and condense thirty-five years into the splitting of money? Where do all the meals I've cooked come in? All the times I've floured chicken in a brown paper bag. The homemade vegetable soup and staying up all night to nurse the girls and Carl back to health while I was sick myself. The waxed linoleum and swept front and back porch. School clothes shopping, groceries in the fridge, light and gas bills mailed on time, the roses planted off-season. Where does all that enter in?

I sat on the couch leafing through my divorce petition. It was nothing more than a form with sparse typing and boxes checked off. ATTORNEY NAME:, ATTORNEY FOR:, COUNTY OF:, PETITIONER: Elaine Cora Browning, RESPONDENT: Carl Dewayne Browning, JUDGMENT (check one box): [ ] Dissolution [ ] Legal Separation [ ] Nullity.

The dissolution box was checked. Only thing left now was to have them delivered. A process server or sheriff would do that. But I wasn't ready yet. The whole thing seemed so final. The lawyer said something to me that stuck in my head: marriage is about love; divorce is about money. I was on the wrong side of the fence. I still loved Carl.

I needed him to tell me why he did it. I didn't care where the telling took place, even if it had to be in court, even if I had to divorce him to hear the truth. I had seen him so clearly in my head. Sitting in the witness stand, telling the judge why he cheated, telling me he was sorry. But it wasn't going to happen. Because somehow fidelity doesn't matter in divorce anymore.

I pulled the only card I had left.

Chapter 17

June 18

I'm beginning to think of love as a can of orange juice concentrate. You start off potent, then you blend in three cans of hopes and desires to perfect taste. Each lie, argument, and disappointment just adds more water and fucks up the flavor.

She wanted to be different than the night before. The kind of girl you take home to your mother, not the kind you think of only when your dick is hard. She wondered how she had lost herself that easily. Being bent and remolded in the dating, breaking-up, and moving-on process. She'd always heard that the older you get, the lower your standards become. She thought she was beyond that, but maybe that's what the whole thing with Eric was about. The official lowering of her expectations of male–female relationships.

Mingus stirred the alfredo sauce with a wooden spoon and turned off the fire. She would be different tonight. Strong not vulnerable. No sex. If Eric was going to like her, he needed to like all of her, not just the part that opened to him like a screaming banshee in heat.

She was afraid her zeal had betrayed her. That her willingness to make love had dropped her standing in his subconscious. She didn't care what Eric said. Maybe he'd overestimated himself. Maybe somewhere inside of him he had to believe her easiness meant something. She was embarrassed. I could have waited past the second date, she thought. But she hadn't.

He arrived at the door, somehow looking better after a long day's work than he had that morning. She let him in. Again he wiped his feet on the doormat and stepped inside. There would be no backsliding tonight.

Mingus took his jacket and laid it over the back of the loveseat. Eric sat a rectangular box with tattered corners on the table and started to unlace his boots.

"Monopoly?" she said with wrinkled forehead.

"Yeah, I stopped home to pick it up, thought maybe I could whip your tail a little bit before dinner."

Mingus smiled but kept her distance. She didn't know how to take him. She had expected him to be all over her before the door was shut good. Eric placed his boots on the side of the couch and sat gap-legged, tapping his fingers on the arm rest.

"I missed you," he said, still tapping.

She didn't like this—the feeling of coming and going at the same time. He was stirring up everything she had managed to settle before he'd gotten there. Slow the pace. No expectations for the future. Just now. Just now, real slow.

She walked over to the couch and sat with her knees angled toward him, the middle cushion between them.

"You know," she said, resting her hands on her knees, trying to look natural, "I did a study on Monopoly when I was in college."

"Really now." Eric ran his middle finger down the outside of her sleeveless arm then clasped his fingers between hers. "It's my favorite game."

"That says a lot about your personality."

"Oh yeah." He kissed the side of her forehead. Her fingers still clasped in his, Eric pulled her closer to him. "What does it tell you about me?"

"Well, I studied ten games, five people per game, all participants between the ages twenty and twenty-five."

"Your results?"

Eric slid her open palm over his lips and kissed into it.

"In my study," she said, averting her eyes from his, "I found a lot of stealing, crooked accounting and bribery going on."

"Get out of here."

"That's what I found. The people who played fair never won."

"It's a game, Mingus. And I'm not a twenty-something kid anymore."

"Well, I just want you to know that I'm still going to date if I want."

"Where did that come from?"

Mingus shrugged her shoulders and leaned back into the couch, unsure of why she felt like a visitor in her own life.

"Is this your way of pushing me away?" he said.

She didn't answer.

"Come here."

Eric raised his arm, motioning for her to slide into him. She wanted to know what it all meant. Each hug, each caress. Every time he smiled at her and took her hand in his. She couldn't take another heartbreak again. Even though everything felt right with him. She'd fallen hard too many times. Seen herself break apart when no one was watching. She couldn't let it happen.

Eric grabbed her waist and molded himself around her.

"Maybe you should go home," Mingus said, her voice muffled in his shoulder.

"Maybe," he said, not loosening his grip, his top lip brushing against her ear, "or maybe I should just hold you like this tonight, until you fall asleep."

Chapter 18

Carl owned several Laundromats, the one in Endsbrook made five. He also dabbled in real estate. Buying, fixing up, and selling for a profit. Managed to make quite a good living for himself. But all I wanted was my house, my own car, and a chance to talk to that cross-toting Jezebel face to face.

The whole idea sounded sick, but I had to go through with it. Walk the same lot Carl walked when he first met her. See what he saw in her. Know why he took her business card with home number and "call me" on the back. I needed to see for myself what made Carl think she was better than me.

I sat across from the dealership in the emerald green Ford Taurus I had rented. I felt like I was going on a first date. I had on my peach linen summer suit and matching bone-colored pumps and purse. Nude knee-highs and clustered pearl earrings with a four-teen-karat flower blooming in the center. I checked my face in the rearview mirror. My forehead was shining. A thin layer of sweat caked the almond beige makeup at my hairline. I flipped open my purse and pulled out my lipstick and powder case.

Brushed the loose beige powder across the bridge of my nose and forehead. Uncapped the lipstick and ran an inch-long streak up both cheeks, then blended in the rose tint with my index and middle finger. I took a last look. My eyes had gone pale green, almost blue, like they always did when I was nervous.

I shut the car door behind me and headed across the street. I spotted her right away. A coffee-colored woman, teaspoon of cream, no sugar. She wore a dark blue skirt suit with six buffed gold buttons lined down the center of her chest. Her hair was different. In the video she wore a short, perfectly rounded afro. I smoothed my hand over my hair. It was still damp from my morning shower. I should have worn it down, shown her that my hair was more hellfire than her lipstick. I was envious of her versatility. Maybe she was wearing a wig—or maybe, the tape was just old and her hair had grown.

My purse hanging at my side, I walked squarely in front of her. She smiled. "May I help you with something?"

"I'm Elaine," I said, staring her in the eye.

"Well, Elaine, what can I do for you today?"

I had played this scenario so many times in my head. Me cursing her out, breaking into tears, trying my best to beat the living daylight out of her. I'd even pictured getting her fired and purchasing my car from her manager as she cleared out her desk. In every one of those situations, she knew who I was.

"Your face looks familiar to me," I said, "I thought maybe we knew each other from somewhere."

"I get that every so often," she said, tapping her clipboard with shrimp-colored nails. "Are you looking for something specific today or are you shopping around?"

The woman was crud. Staring me straight in the eye, tapping her clipboard like I was wasting her time.

"I'm here to purchase a car."

"Great," she said. "New vehicles are on this lot and we have some very reasonably priced preowns on our adjacent lot. I can walk you over and introduce you to Chuck if you like."

"Excuse me, you did say your name was Gladys, right?"

"Glenda," she said, enunciating each syllable, "Glenda Stewart."

"I'm interested in that one," I said, pointing my finger like a Russian roulette bottle to a cream two-door. "I'd like a test drive."

"Right this way."

She unbuttoned her blazer and placed it on the back seat. Her full breasts curved loosely against a black silk chemise. It was low cut, just like the blouse she'd worn in the video, only this time I could tell she wasn't wearing a bra. I wondered if her bralessness was a marketing tool. If that's how she'd caught Carl's attention. He'd always liked nice-size breasts. He used to tell me my body reminded him of a black woman's when we were young. Ripe and firm, soft in the right places. He especially liked my behind, said I had just the right amount of stuffing. I would be flattered. Especially after leaving my family, I used to feel like I belonged someplace when he said those things. Now it just seems like I was a stand-in. That at a certain point a reminder wasn't good enough and he needed the real thing.

"As you can see," Glenda said in standard salesperson demeanor, "the accessories are designed for driver comfort. Everything you need is within arm's reach."

"Are you married?" I asked, staring at the road ahead, my fingers clutched around the steering wheel.

"Excuse me?"

I clutched my fingers tighter.

"Are you married; do you have any children?"

Glenda thought for a moment, then crossed her arms over her chest.

"Why do you ask?" she said.

"I like to know something about the people I do business with, makes me feel more comfortable."

Glenda stared. I looked at her through the side of my eye.

"To answer your question, I've never been married and I have two children."

"Never thought about marrying?"

She breathed hard. I could hear it under the hum of the air-conditioning.

"Thought about," she tapped her finger on her arm, "I'm still thinking about it. You can make a right there at the stop sign and make a U-turn in the cul-de-sac."

I surrendered a short glance but couldn't smile. I was sitting next to the woman who was coveting my husband.

"Someone in particular?"

"Come again," she said.

"Are you looking to marry someone particular or do you just want to get married?"

"I've definitely met the one," she said.

"That's the same thing I said when I met my husband. Almost thirty-five years ago."

Glenda snapped her fingers. "That's what I'm talking about. I love to hear success stories."

She seemed happy for me. I looked over and caught her smile. It was real. A part of me thought the whole thing had to be a really bad misunderstanding. She couldn't be talking about Carl. Carl was my husband. And the man of her dreams had to be someone else. But I had a video and the letters. A business card with her name and home number. I wanted all those things to be lies. I wanted to laugh with this woman about our separate loves and drive home in my new car to my husband. I wanted that more than anything.

•   •   •

I followed Glenda through double glass doors, past the reception-ist counter to a small square room with closed blinds.

"How does this sound?" she said, pushing a worksheet toward me, clicking her shoe on and off her heel.

"I went to the bank this morning; I'm paying cash."

"Thirty-eight thousand dollars plus tax and license? You're pay-ing that today?"

"Yes."

Glenda's voice was steady, but she clicked her heel faster.

"If you'll give me your license and Social Security card, I'll have you out of here in no time."

I unsnapped my purse and pulled my Social Security card and driver's license from my wallet.

"Sign here, please."

She slid her clipboard toward me. I signed and slid it back to her with my IDs secured under the metal clip. Glenda picked up the paper and smiled. Then she looked down at the signature.

"Elaine Browning," she said pensively, more to herself than to me. "Elaine Browning? You told me O'Brien."

"That's my maiden name. I go by that sometimes."

Glenda kept her eyes glued on the signature. "Elaine Browning."

"Is something wrong?"

"Your name just reminds me of someone, that's all. I'll be right back."

I watched Glenda rise from the small desk.

"Who does it remind you of?" I questioned.

"It's nothing." She shook her head. "For a brief moment I thought you were someone, but clearly you're not her, she's uh, well, you're not her."

"She's what?"

"The woman I'm referring to is a black woman and clearly you're not black."

"No, I'm not black." I laughed, Glenda joining in. "No, I'm definitely not black." I stopped laughing. "Did he ever tell you I was black?"

"Excuse me?"

"Carl. Did he ever tell you I was black? You know Carl Browning, the married man you've been fucking and giving cards to for the last year. Did he ever tell you I was black or did you assume I was because he is?"

"Excuse me for a moment."

"No you don't." I stood up. "You're not going anywhere until you hear me out."

"I think you need to take this up with Carl."

"No, I'm taking this up with you. How do you go on fucking another woman's husband for over a year? Did you ever think about what you were doing? Did you ever think about the fact that he's been married for thirty-five years?"

"I'm not the villain here, Elaine." Glenda put her hand on her hip. "This situation didn't take place in a vacuum. Things were bad between the two of you before I ever met Carl."

"It *didn't* take place in a vacuum. Did you ever stop to think about the fact that he has a family? Besides me, did you think about his daughters? Do you think they're going to be sitting across from you at Christmas dinners or that you'll ever be invited to family gatherings? This situation isn't just about you and Carl—now who's operating in a damn vacuum?"

Glenda reached for the phone.

"I think Carl needs to get down here before this gets out of control."

"It's already out of control. And what the fuck is Carl going to do? Pull me out of here?"

"You need to leave, miss, this is my place of business."

"I'm not your miss. I'm *Mrs.* Browning, and if you think for a second that you and Carl are about to stroll off into happiness after everything I've been through, or that Carl is going to have a pot to piss in after this, you are sadly mistaken."

"That's why black men shouldn't marry white women," she said smugly. "It may have taken thirty-five years, but you're just another white trash gold digger."

"Oh, and you're justified because I'm white? It was a black woman's husband you thought you were fucking, remember? What does that make you?"

"I love Carl."

"Bullshit. I gave up my family to marry Carl. My family. I haven't seen my mother in thirty-five years. Do you know what that's like? I've sacrificed everything for him and I've never slept with another man or taken anything from him. You don't have an inch of the integrity I have. And if I didn't mind sitting in jail for a few days I would beat your ass."

"You ain't beatin' shit up in here. I'm going to call Carl and tell him exactly what you're doing."

"Call him. Call him right now." I pushed the receiver into her face. "Let him know that I'm buying the car that I sacrificed for and should have had thirty-five years ago. Tell him that his girlfriend bitch won't be making any commission on it—tell him that he's lost the best thing that ever happened to him."

I walked out of the office and pleaded with myself not to start crying. I stopped at the reception desk and asked for the sales manager. A tall, balding man with a graying beard came to the desk.

"Yes, I'm here to purchase a car."

"Have you been working with someone?"

"Yes, but that woman has been fucking my husband and I am *not* buying anything from her. I have cash. Either you can help me right now and sign something guaranteeing she won't get commission, or I'll take my business elsewhere."

"No problem, ma'am. Right this way, I'll finalize your agreement personally."

Chapter 19

June 20

White fingers don't feel any different. With your eyes closed, a touch is a touch. It's seeing your future in the wrong man's eyes that's the hard part.

They lay up on the couch, his knee sandwiched between her thighs, her bra unfastened underneath her blouse. Their bodies sank into rust-colored cushions that gave under their collective weight, their legs spilling onto the floor.

Skirt bunched around her waist, his fingers pressed her clitoris through a thin layer of white cotton. She relaxed under his fingers, let him massage the tension between her legs, the fear in her heart. She wanted him to touch her. He could make her better. Make it easy to string her heart between two men. Man No. 1—Monday, Wednesday, Friday, Saturday. Man No. 2—Thursday, Sunday. Tuesday—self. She had it figured out. Head tilted back, soft kisses on her neck, Steven slid his hand into her underwear. She was warm against his fingers.

"I'm hot," Mingus said, pulling his hand from between her legs.

"Something wrong?"

"I just need some air."

Mingus jumped up from the couch and straightened her skirt as she walked over to the window. She stood there, the window closed, staring at the abandoned field across the chain-link fence. She wondered if jasmine was blooming.

"Mingus, are you okay?"

"Yeah, I just uh, I'm a little tired."

She held her breast through the outside of her shirt. Her nipples were still sensitive. Steven came up behind her and placed his arms around her waist.

"I apologize," he said.

"For what?"

"Moving too fast. I didn't mean to make you uncomfortable."

"It wasn't you, Steven. I'm trippin'."

"You want to talk about it?"

Mingus turned slightly and looked at Steven from out of the corner of her eye. His eyes were still kind, just like they had been at the restaurant. "No," she said, "I just need some sleep."

"I'll call you tomorrow then."

"Sounds good."

Steven adjusted his uniform before he walked outside. Mingus stood still at the window. Didn't check to see if he had locked the bottom lock behind him. She thought about the jasmine. Wondered if Eric liked the smell as much as she did.

Chapter 20

I drove home. I didn't feel, I don't remember seeing anything. I just heard a rattling in my head. The sales manager gave me the keys and I walked out. Handed him $40,000 and walked out. And somehow I thought there would be victory in the rendering of that money. My blood was on it. But it could have been a hundred thousand dollars and it wouldn't have felt any different.

Something in me would have sworn, pulling that money out of the bank, large bills in my name, stuffing them into that envelope, something in me would have sworn this was all I needed to do to love myself again. But what I was looking for I couldn't find in money. And that's when I cried. Not till then.

I was broken. Not like anything specific, but like everything that breaks and looks fine on the outside. When you shake them, all you hear is a miscellaneous rattle. Something rolling around misplaced on the inside. I was all those broken things, all at once. So much so it numbed me. And I don't remember anything else. Not putting the keys in the ignition or closing the door. All I can say is that at some point, the rattling got so loud I died. Not physically, not all of me, but the vital part. Something just beyond my heart that ticks louder and closer than heartbeat.

Chapter 21

July 18

For me, losing love was more compelling than having it. Now I stare happiness in the face, holding on, wondering if I look away, how long it would take to disappear.

She exited the two-lane highway and turned left past the Pump n' Go station on the corner. It was Saturday, boys playing stickball in the street. Girls licking on Popsicles waiting for their turn at Chinese jump rope. Mingus was thinking about Eric. How he'd stood by her through all her moods—her fears. They had become something over the past few weeks. And despite her trying to push him away, he was still there.

Amidst all the street activity, Eva stuck out. She sat gap-legged on the stoop in some Daisy Duke shorts, sipping on a bottle of orange Crush.

Mingus reached over and unlocked the door. She eyed Eva's lime green tank top with two strings crisscrossing around her waist.

"I see you're keeping cool today," Mingus said.

"And I see you still consider cut-off jogging shorts high fashion." Eva got in and closed the door behind her. "Where's the rental car at?"

"The Lexus dealership on Third."

"M'Dea just left it there?"

Eva fastened her seat belt and propped her right foot, tennis shoe and all, on the dashboard.

"Yeah, do you have to do that?"

"My leg's cramped up. What she buy?"

"Do you have a cramp every time you get in my car?"

"Anyway, what she buy?"

"SC Four hundred Coupe."

"Hey, all right, all right," Eva said, dancing to a tune in her head and snapping her fingers. "I'm gonna have to check it out."

"Just don't try to borrow it; she just got it."

"And when you become my mama I'll listen to you."

Luckily the dealership was only ten minutes from Eva's apartment. Mingus was glad she had rolled down the windows before picking her up; the air-conditioning only helped circulate Eva's perfume, which was always too loud. A few seconds into the silence Mingus turned on the radio.

"Ooh, that's my song, turn it up," Eva said, pumping her shoulders and pushing her flattened palms into the air. "Whoop, whoop!"

Every song was her song. She wiggled her behind all the way to the dealership. That's what Mingus liked most about being around Eva. Her energy. She could find fun in a toothpick.

They parked across the street from the dealership behind the emerald green Ford Taurus M'Dea had left there the day before.

"You know what she looks like?" Eva asked, looking Mingus dead in the eye.

"M'Dea said she was tall with honey blond hair. An asymmetrical haircut."

"Sounds like she trying to be cute." Eva turned up her lip.

"I guess." Mingus cut her eyes in high attitude. Sometimes she could really tell they were sisters. Times like these when it was them fighting against the world instead of each other.

"I want to scope her out, see what she trying to do. M'Dea still trippin' off the fact that she's black?"

"Yeah," Mingus said, turning off the engine. "I can't even explain the look she gave me the last time I saw her. Like all of a sudden she realized I was black or something."

"She knew that when you were born."

Eva smacked her lips.

"This was different," Mingus said, "like she realized I was closer in genetic makeup to Dad's mistress than to her."

"Is that what you think?"

"What do mean?"

Eva turned toward Mingus, her foot still on the dashboard.

"Do you think you're more black than white?"

"Basically," Mingus said.

"Well, at least you ain't trying to be a white girl with black skin. I've tried that one and the shit don't work. If M'Dea would have married a white man, I'd be a hell of a lot better off."

"Are you saying you wish you weren't black?" Mingus asked.

"I'm saying I wish I had a job. White skin would make it that much easier."

"Well, M'Dea has white skin and look at her. I'm still tripping off the fact that she came down here to this woman's job."

"She didn't just come down, she locked horns with this be-yatch."

"You know she served Daddy with divorce papers when he got home, right?"

"What? You lyin'." Eva put her hands on her hip and stared at Mingus. "Damn, M'Dea put fifty on it. Go, Elaine. It's your birthday, it's your birthday! Get busy! It's your . . ."

None of this was good. Mingus knew that after all the drama had settled, the deterioration of her family would remain. She thought about the remnants of a verse she'd heard in church one Easter when she was little. Something about father against son, mother against daughter. A house divided against itself.

"You want to drive the rental car and I'll follow you to return it?"

"That's cool," Eva said, "you know what though, I need to go pick up some incense and stuff afterward. I can just drop it off and catch the bus home."

"You sure?"

"Yeah, girl. I got some errands to take care of. Plus, the owner of the incense shop is hella fine. He's Muslim though. Orthodox. I'm gonna peep him out a little bit."

"All right," Mingus said. "Here's the key, I'm gonna go then."

"Wait, we gotta check out Miss Thang." Eva gave Mingus a you-can-leave-after-that look.

"I'm not going over to that car lot, Eva."

"You ain't no fun." Eva snatched the key from Mingus's hand. "Let's just stand by the rental car for a few minutes, so she'll know we're on her back."

"See what I have on?"

"Ain't nobody gonna see you up close. Come on, shit."

Eva jumped out of the car and headed toward the rental car. Mingus followed apprehensively behind her.

They leaned against the driver's side window, glass warm against their backs, arms crossed over ample chests they'd both inherited from their mother.

"Listen," Mingus said, Eva's shoulder resting against her bare arm, "a good friend of mine is looking for a production assistant and I told him about you."

"A production assistant?" Eva said, still browsing the lot for Glenda.

"Yeah, I just thought you might be interested. It's in television, it pays well."

"I'll try it," she said, still looking ahead.

"I'll leave his number on your answering machine then."

"There she goes!"

Eva grabbed Mingus's arm.

Glenda wore a black pantsuit with gold cuffs and a pointed gold collar.

"That suit is bad, but that blonde-ass hair gotta go. You know it's a weave."

Mingus didn't commit. Just wondered why her father chose her. She looked so different than M'Dea.

Glenda walked from car to car with a thirty-something black man at her side. Every so often she would glance over in their direction. Eva suggested they stay long enough for Glenda to internalize their presence. Mingus wondered, even if she did know who they were, if she cared.

"She cares. We're Carl's daughters," Eva said. "Women know in the long run if they can't get in with a man's daughters things are harder for them."

"Sounds like experience talking. I'm gonna go."

"Cool," Eva said, letting her remark slide.

Chapter 22

I walked over to the kitchen sink and lathered dishwashing liquid between my palms. Softly, I scrubbed salty mascara from my cheeks. My eyes were red, and it felt like there were a thousand tiny grains of sand under my lids. I wiped my hands with a dish towel and stared at my reflection in the bay window. White curtains with yellow frill framed my face. Sun bounced in making a glare of my eyes. I had to laugh. After everything I had been through in my life, I had finally arrived at the bottom. The bottom of whatever game it was that I had forgotten I was playing.

I thought I had won a long time ago—at least by the time I was pregnant with his child, if not then when I left my family and we got married, if not then when I bore both his children and made a home for us. It made me laugh to know that it was never over, not until now.

As I turned off the water, I could hear the faint click of his key in the front lock. Even though I knew it was over in my heart, a sting of tension tightened my belly. I took six steps to the kitchen table. I sat there, patting the last drops of water from my face.

Carl dropped his keys on the coffee table. His feet tracked with a premeditated slowness into the kitchen.

"You finally did it," he said walking toward me, both hands in pocket, stopping when his gray slacks grazed the edge of the table. "Are you happy?"

No answer.

"I can't believe how ungrateful you are. I gave you everything you could ask for and you messed it up."

I stared up at him. His eyes scolded me. I wanted to throw the bowl of oranges on the table at him.

"Oh, now you can't talk, huh. You've been spreading our business to strangers all day and now you can't talk."

"Bullshit." I tasted a concentration of acid in my throat. "How did you hear about it Carl, from a stranger?"

"I never dreamed," he said chopping air, his erect palm accentuating his words, "I never dreamed you would do this to me. Steal money and act like a damn fool at people's place of employment. You destroyed my savings."

"Strangers, people's? What truck do you think I fell off of? You're mad because I confronted that woman and now you're found out. How long has it been, Carl? A year? More? You may as well tell me."

"You don't know what you are talking about. How could you steal from me, Elaine?"

"It wasn't stealing when I bought those slacks you have on or when you took that bitch to movies on our credit card—but it's stealing when I buy myself something I should have bought a long time ago?"

"I earned that money." He slammed his hand down on the table.

"And I took care of you for thirty-five years while you earned it. I deserve every penny I spent and a hell of a lot more."

"The car is going back."

"The car's staying right where I parked it."

"Give me the keys."

He walked over to me, his thigh pressing my shoulder.

"Don't touch me, Carl. You're gonna pay for more than a car if you touch me."

"Gold digger."

He took a step back. His Adam's apple bobbed up and down.

"Did you get that catchy phrase from your girlfriend?"

His face contorted. Lines squeezed into the tight space between his eyes. His eyebrows pushed against the lines like bookends.

"You've ruined my life. You realize that, don't you?"

"How did I ruin your life?"

He didn't want to say it. He stood there with his arms clenched over his chest. His eyes were tearing from how badly he wanted to hurt me.

"You're pathetic, you know that," I said. "I ruined *your* life. That's a joke. I gave up everything for you. I was eighteen, Carl. I don't even know if my parents are still alive."

"You're never going to let me forget that, are you, Elaine? You've given up so much for me. Do you ever think about what I gave up?"

Tears started to roll warm down my cheeks.

"I gave up my dream—a normal black life, with a normal black wife and black children. I just want to be like everybody else. Not have to put on shows or have my defenses up when I'm out with my wife. I get tired."

"So you cheated because you wished you had a normal life? You never had to ask me to marry you."

"You were pregnant, Ellie."

"I was pregnant because we had sex. Don't blame thirty-five years of marriage on me because I got pregnant. I didn't trap you."

"I felt trapped."

There. Carl had done it. For the first time in my life, I heard him say what I always knew he had felt. I watched his lips twist out words that landed squarely in my chest. I didn't care if he watched me fall apart. I wanted him to see. See the impact of a lifetime of lies and cover-ups. How was I ever supposed to believe he loved me again? How could I think back on memories that had been so sweet to me and smile? I sat back in the chair and folded in like a collapsing box.

"I just felt trapped, that's all." Carl threw up his hands. "You remember what it was like. I couldn't just leave you and let you go back home to your father. He wanted to kill you and me both. I wasn't raised like that. I had to take care of mine and that's what I've been doing."

The whole marriage had been him taking care of his. It was supposed to change.

"Do you love me, Carl?"

"Don't ask that."

"Did you ever love me?"

"I respected you. Appreciated how much you loved our family." He looked at me and shook his head.

"Damnit, Ellie. I've tried to make it work. There's just been so much. Working, trying to support the family, putting Mingus through school, keeping the businesses going. I just think we got caught up. You in this house. You keep a better house than my mama kept. Raising the kids. We've never been friends, Ellie. She didn't just catch my eye, she caught all of me. We talk about stuff. Anything. Home repairs, news articles, salsa dancing, anything. We can relate to each other. She understands—"

"I can't relate? What, because she's black and I'm not?"

"Yeah. Racism's not dead, Ellie. If I can live the rest of my life with less of it, I—"

"I don't want to hear it."

"You never wanted to hear it. You've never wanted to understand what it means to be a black person in this country. That humanist shit only goes so far. And every time I've tried to tell you the real deal, you shut me up. Well, be damn sure my girls know what the truth is. At least Mingus."

He grabbed my hand.

"Don't leave, Ellie, I just want you to understand. This didn't just happen out of nowhere. I've done everything I could think to. Don't I have the right to be happy?"

I shook my head. I felt like tired cobwebs were falling down over me. I wanted to disappear. Ball up like a dirty rag under the sink.

"It doesn't matter," I said.

"It does matter, at least to me."

Carl pulled a chair out from under the table and sat next to me.

"I didn't want it this way. It'll be thirty-five years in October. The thirteenth. Three months away, Ellie, this seemed like the lesser of two evils."

"An affair seemed right to you?"

"It's not just an affair, Ellie. I just thought—"

He stopped himself. He leaned in toward my face, trying to connect with my eyes. I looked nowhere specific, almost like I wasn't looking at all.

"I didn't think you could survive by yourself. You've never been by yourself. And this way you could keep the house; I could come around every now and then, mow the lawn, make sure everything is working okay."

My vision refocused. I was staring at the pale green refrigerator.

"You're talking like you still want this to happen."

"What would we lose?" Carl turned my face toward his. "Our family would still be together. We haven't had a real husband–wife relationship in a long time; not that much would change."

I looked him in the eye.

"You're crazy."

"Think about it, Ellie. You could even have your own account if that type of thing is important to you. We could make it look however you want it to."

"I married you, Carl, so that I could have a husband. Not an arrangement. Not a checking account. I still . . ."

I couldn't break down again. I sucked up all of the energy I had left and got up from the table. I pulled a manila envelope from the bill organizer next to the refrigerator.

"They told me I should have someone other than myself give these to you, but I could never find the right time. You should get them from me anyway."

I handed him the envelope.

He didn't want to take it. I sat the papers in the empty napkin holder.

"Divorce papers?"

"Take them, Carl. We've been through enough already."

"I just never thought—"

"What, that I'd look after my best interests?"

"It's over," he said, like he was just now catching on. It seemed strange.

"It's been over."

"I don't know what to say."

He looked up at me.

I walked out of the kitchen to the bedroom and closed the door behind me. At some point, he showed himself out.

Chapter 23

July 13
I keep you hidden
like period-stained panties
and letters from old lovers
You are in me
Your name written across my wrists
in umbilical cord dust
I show you to Jesus
ask why I have your eyes
ask why I cry backwards
backwash forgiveness on my tongue
I am stuck outside your womb
trying to get back in
trying to match the laugh lines
around your heart when he's with you
You traded me
for black-eyed dreams
and TJ Swan paper cup apologies
big hands
over
small hugs
and sometimes
late at night
I still miss your kiss
on my forehead

Mingus remembered. Seeing through walls when she was younger. Matching her memory to her parents' words and pitch. By eleven years old she had them down pat. She knew that the worst arguments started at the dinner table and ended on the front porch.

Dinnertime would come and everything would seem normal at first. The chairs at the head and foot of the table would be empty as usual. M'Dea would spend her last few minutes in the kitchen finishing up the food. Eva would make too-sweet Kool-Aid or a pitcher of iced tea with floating orange and lemon slices visible through the glass. It was Mingus's job to set the table. She would place a plate and cup on each of the four muted-yellow plastic mats then arrange a knife, fork, and spoon on a folded square paper napkin. Waiting for the rest of the family to take their seats, she would doodle in her diary or write down stray thoughts until dinner was ready.

Instead of sitting next to M'Dea, as he normally did, sometimes Carl would place himself next to Mingus. Mingus knew it was trouble. Patterns and routines were how the family identified each other. Talking was secondary. Tertiary. If instead of making a ham and cheese sandwich with a tad of strawberry preserve after walking home from school, Eva went directly to her room, something was wrong. If M'Dea woke up at five A.M. and had cereal, milk, and fruit on the table instead of bacon, eggs, and grits, something was wrong. So when her father sat in the wrong seat, Mingus pretended not to notice. She'd pretended to focus all her attention on writing in her diary, and bit by bit, she'd scoot herself as far away from her father as she could.

One by one M'Dea would bring four filled dishes from the kitchen and sit them next to the pitcher of iced tea and hot-water cornbread in the center of the table. As M'Dea walked back and forth through the brown swinging doors that separated the kitchen from the dining room, Mingus wouldn't look up. She didn't have to. Her memory told her that M'Dea's back was growing pristinely erect and her eyes were starting to water. Mingus would write slowly as if in deepest meditation. She didn't react to Eva's not quite stifled giggles or how the table shook from Eva's foot tapping the leg of her chair in nervous anticipation.

After grace, Mingus would pile on more food than normal on these nights in hopes that M'Dea wouldn't be upset by Carl's public boycott of her food. As everyone else at the table dug into scalloped potatoes or chicken with homemade dumplings, Carl would crunch on seasoned pork rinds out of an oil-stained paper bag and wash them down with Coca-Cola in a thick-bottomed glass bottle. He was playing dirty and Mingus would feel sorry for her mother. Refusing M'Dea's food was like refusing her, and no one in the house had the courage to do it, except Carl.

When finished with his Coke and rinds, he would ball up the paper bag with both hands, plop it down onto his clean plate, and wordlessly dismiss himself from the table. M'Dea would watch his back until he was completely out of sight, then she'd pick up her barely eaten plate of food and flee into the kitchen. Mingus could hear the crying, even though M'Dea tried to hide it behind the rush of running water from the kitchen sink. Many times, Mingus had imagined herself bursting through the swinging doors and wrapping her arms around M'Dea's waist to console her. She never did though, even though sometimes she almost made it out of her seat. In her heart, she wasn't sure her mother wanted her consolation. M'Dea had Eva, and what they shared together seemed real. Mingus envied Eva in that respect. Eva didn't have to think about whether or not to go to M'Dea, she just could. Carl could too, even after the worst disagreement. They'd often end up on the front porch, making up over a bottle of Night Train or TJ Swan. Mingus wouldn't sleep during those late-night makeups. She'd lay in bed atop her blankets listening to them through the partially opened window. She should have felt happy for them, but the more she heard her mother giggle like a love-crazed teenager, and the more intricate the old stories they replayed, the sadder she felt. M'Dea seemed happiest during those times. Like she finally had her husband all to herself. Like the burden of sharing had faded with Mingus's ten o'clock summer curfew. And in those moments of disconnection, as Mingus lay in bed with the sweetness of butterscotch staining her tongue, she wiped the tears from her baby doll's face.

Chapter 24

I couldn't get up from the table. Knew Ellie wasn't coming back, but I couldn't bring myself to unlock my knees and go. I heard the door close just as firm. She wasn't coming back. Wasn't 'bout to apologize or ask what she could do to make me stay. Musta been the only time in my life where I was really knowing what fear was. I could feel it creeping on up the back side of my legs. She was moving on and it didn't make no difference what I was doing. She had made up her mind. I could see it in her stare, green eyes all afire, even behind the tears. Didn't even have to touch her to feel it. I don't know, maybe I shoulda been happy that she knew how to get along without me. I'da never thought it though.

And that's what stole my thunder. Ellie and I been tied at the hip for a lot of years. All this time I've been knowing that she needed me. How was I supposed to know that I needed her too? Something in me wasn't feeling right. I was missing something without her love, something that disappeared the moment I knew she could take it away. Realized she was the only thing I ever knew was gone be there no matter what.

Much as I love Glenda, Glenda and Ellie do something different to a man. Ellie makes me feel needed. Glenda makes me
feel like I can need her. And when you get that from a woman,
that you can need her, then you can let your guard down some
and just be yourself. I've been wanting to be myself for a long
time.

I shoulda been happy sitting up there at that table with them
divorce papers in my hand. I was finally free. Didn't have to pretend no more. Didn't have to live no double life. I could just go
home to Glenda and unpack my bags for real this time. Put all my
clothes in that closet she said was mine a long time ago. Change
my mail. Park my car in the garage instead of at the curb. I'd been
waiting to do all these things and now I wasn't sure.

Then I started to think maybe my problem wasn't with Ellie.
Maybe I really did love her as much as I'd always known she loved
me. Maybe my problem was with myself. I never could get over
the fact that she got pregnant. I was all of twenty-two, in my
prime. The military was paying my travel ticket and I was willing to go. After seeing Paris, I was thinking about givin' 'em
another four years. I met Ellie on a pit stop. Had never thought
of marriage, more less a baby. Everyone knew that a man in
green uniform stuck less than snow on sunshine. A good meal and
good sex, that was all I was looking for and all I was willing to
offer.

And Ellie. I was liking on her, but not enough to have babies.
She was 'bout to graduate from high school, was thinking about
going into nursing or to secretarial school. I wasn't thinking she
wanted to get tied down. Not with no black man. Not in America. Paris or something was different, not that different, but different all the same. I had never known no white girl, Irish, to be
interested in me, not on U.S. soil. I was flattered. Thought we
were both being curious.

Our first time was in the barracks. She made her way around to the NCO Club and I was sittin' outside waitin'. Saturday night. I walked off first, she followed twenty or so steps behind. 12:00 P.M. Early enough so that the guys would still be out.

Second time she got pregnant. We didn't know it at first. Not till afterwards when I pulled off the condom and noticed that there was barely fluid in it. I never even heard it pop. That's what made me wonder about her. She got up from my lower bunk, straightened out her clothes, and walk herself out. Quick. Never once looked me in the eye. All that night I sat up in my bunk wanting to scream. *She trapped me. Pinned a hole in the condom and trapped me.*

I had seven months left. Part of me wanted to reenlist right away. Get out of town scot-free. But I was knowing she was pregnant. Even though I didn't see her for three months. Even before she showed up to tell me. I was knowing. I was going to be a father and I wasn't ready to be a husband. So I sacrificed, did what Mama said I was supposed to do. Bought Elaine a bus pass, and when my time was up, I headed home to be with her. Back to being a small-town boy living in my mother's house. But this time with a family of my own.

I never got used to that. Even when we moved into our own small place, even when we bought our first house. A part of me knew I was supposed to be doing something different with my life. That there was another wife out there I was supposed to marry. A wife who got tired of waiting on me and married someone else. All this I knew like my own heartbeat, and I tucked it deep inside. Tried to forget about it.

Glenda was my second chance. How was I supposed to let my life slip by me twice? I couldn't. I didn't have the will to. Only thing I didn't expect was that even with my new life, I would still want my old one. My kids would always be mine, I had raised them, but not my wife. That's when I realized I wanted them both. The woman who needed me and the woman I needed. My thirty-five-year marriage and the hope of happiness with somebody else.

That's why I couldn't leave that table. Maybe Elaine was as important to my happiness as Glenda was. Different sides of the same coin. My wives in two completely different lives, joined together by my indecision.

Chapter 25

July 24
There are no secrets.

She wondered where he'd find it. Her infidelity. Her toppling of commitment like kindergarten blocks. Covers pulled to her throat, she lay in the darkness of twilight counting the shadows on the wall.

It would be in her eyes. One night when he stared too deep or she cried a little too long. It would be a subtle exchange. Fitting snug like a tourniquet around his heart, then slowly taking away his breath.

First he'd ask what, then why, then sit in imperfect silence, fumbling through answers that would never be good enough. Sit in silence that told her she better not touch him.

She lay there watching the trees, darkness coating their limbs. She didn't know why she did it. Fear is the only thing that seemed real that night. Like maybe she'd have a chance with Eric if she could give part of herself to Steven. Not care too much, love too much, need him too much. Like another man could bring balance to her spirit.

What was I thinking, Mingus thought, fighting back the tears.

A part of her wanted to rationalize it—stick with grade school definitions of relationship. *He didn't ask me to be his girlfriend yet. We're just dating, we're not going steady.* None of that mattered. She wanted to be his girlfriend, more than his girlfriend. She wanted to wake up every morning with her head on his chest. She wanted to come home late at night and smell his white cheddar popcorn scenting her apartment. She wanted takeout for two and both their deodorants in the medicine cabinet. She wanted him to love her.

She grabbed the phone from the nightstand and sat it on her stomach. She tried to convince herself that it would be better not to call, that she should tell Steven in person. Maybe if he stared her in the eye he would be able to see the sincerity of her conflict and not hate her for it.

"Hi, sorry to call you so late."

"Mingus," he said, sounding like he was awakened from sleep. "I'm just glad you returned my calls finally. Are you all right?"

She placed her hand over her eyes and shook her head.

"Yeah. I just wanted to apologize for the other night, I—"

"Mingus, I told you it's okay. I should have taken things slower. I should be apologizing to you."

"Steven, just listen to me, please. I'm sorry because—I started dating someone."

"Whoa," he said.

There was silence.

"I'm sorry; I should have told you a little sooner."

"Keith?"

"Someone new."

He let out a heavy breath.

"A black guy, I take it."

"Yeah."

"Whew. I thought we were starting something, but I guess I was wrong."

"I don't know what to say. We were starting something. It's just, I like you a lot, but culturally, I—"

"You don't have to explain," he said, his demeanor growing colder.

"I feel like I do. There's a coffee shop on Sycamore and First that's open late. Corbin's. We could talk."

"Mingus, really, what's there to talk about? You prefer black men, you told me that from the beginning."

Mingus flipped the blanket off of her body and pulled a pair of jeans from the pile of clothes next to the bed.

"Just meet me, please. Or I can come over to your place."

"I don't see the point."

"Please, Steven."

He breathed hard.

"Give me thirty. I'll meet you there."

Chapter 26

I met Glenda at the Laundromat. It was a Sunday evening and I was cleaning out lint trays in the dryers, about to wash down the counters for closing. I was friendly to her, but no more friendly than I woulda been to any other patron. It was my first full week of business and I was needing to build me a steady clientele. I treated everybody like a patron. Even folks passing through to get change or use the restroom.

I went about my business and didn't notice her much until she spoke to me. Asked me if I could get her tennis shoes from wrapped around the agitator blades in the wash machine, the strings had gotten all knotted up. I obliged and in the process of getting the mess untangled we started up a conversation.

She's a beautiful full-bodied woman but the first thing I noticed on her was her voice, a soothing alto. Kind of voice that makes you relax just listening to it. Just the right amount of base and melody. We stood there shootin' the shit for a while. I decided to pull up one of the folding chairs and make myself comfortable. My knees aren't so good anymore and I'd been standing up the better part of the day.

I watched the way she folded clothes. Watched how she pulled one piece out of the dryer at a time, shook it out, then folded and tucked all the corners so everything had the same shape. Ellie would take a big pile of clothes, drop it onto the couch, and fold it into assorted shapes and sizes. Glenda's way seemed fresh and new.

We chatted like we were old friends or family. I felt comfortable around her. She told me about the small house she'd just bought and how her son was finally starting to adjust to his new neighborhood. She'd never married the boy's father. When I asked why, all she said was he wasn't the marrying type. Took her all of getting pregnant to figure that out. And as much as I tried not to, I couldn't help thinking of Ellie. Couldn't she see that I wasn't the marrying type either back then? I admired Glenda, she didn't need to trap a man into loving her. She didn't need to be married to feel secure about herself.

That's when I told her about Ellie. Said that somewhere down the line we stopped fittin'. We'd sit in the same room with each other for hours, her knitting, me catching a game or reading a fishing magazine, and we'd never say a word or even look at each other.

Glenda said it was like having a favorite sweater. When you first buy it, you wear it all the time. Special gatherings you wear it. Lazy afternoons you wear it. It seems to fit every occasion. As time passes on, you stop giving it the special attention it used to get. But you still love it and it holds a special place in your heart. After several years, you start to wonder where that old pink-and-blue sweater went to. You start looking for it, try to remember that last time you wore it, if you tucked it away somewhere or if someone had borrowed it. Eventually you find it in the garage, taped up in a box. You take the sweater into the bedroom to try it on. It seems like all of a sudden it doesn't fit anymore. It's tight where it used to be loose, loose where it used to fit just right. You find that moths have eaten through the sleeves and that one of the shoulder pads is missing. It just doesn't seem to be the same sweater you fell in love with ages ago. And in reality, it isn't. As time changed you, it changed the sweater as well, and no one saw the metamorphosis until it was too late.

Her story made sense to me. She had put words to something I'd been feeling for a long time. As she packed up her clothes into her laundry bag that night, all I could think about was how badly I wanted to go with her. Instead I said goodbye like a gentleman and pretended I wasn't hoping when I took her business card.

Chapter 27

August 7

I almost did. We were nude. He got aroused as he brushed my hair, my head was in his lap. I wanted to. I could smell his scent. But my mouth is virgin and I want to keep it that way.

She had waited long enough. Waited for him to call. Waited for him to stop by and tell her he needed to talk. That's what she expected from her father, for him to deal with her on the level. He had always dealt with her on the level. Even when she was a child.

They used to sit together on the back porch. Denim-ed knees touching. A wooden bowl of shiny brown pecans sitting at their feet. Mingus would have a ribbed metal nut cracker in hand. He would use his teeth or the heel of his boot. She could sit there for hours with him. They'd exchange stories as they chewed on pecans. She'd talk about Eva or her classmates; he'd talk about work or a misunderstanding he'd had with M'Dea. Real stuff, hard stuff even, that was how they'd dealt with each other.

But what if he could stop loving her? What if distance and time could make them little more than cards mailed on birthdays? She was afraid of that. That one day she would realize that breaking pecans on the back porch happened in a different lifetime. Maybe in a dream.

• • •

The silver-framed glass door swung open and instantly her nostrils filled with the smell of laundry detergent and fabric softener. Two long rows of washers ran the length of the room. Round glass-faced dryers lined the left wall. A woman leafed through a hair magazine as she waited for her clothes to dry. Mingus walked past the woman down the dryer-lined aisle, toward the back office. The door was locked. Mingus knocked. She'd seen his car in the parking lot, he had to be in there. She knocked again then pressed her shoulder into the door. The door gave way, her father had opened it.

They stood facing each other, manufacturing pregnant silence under a hum of rotating dryers. He looked different. Like a blown fuse had short-circuited the laughter in his eyes. Mingus touched his face. She couldn't believe she'd been mad at him, especially after looking into his eyes. They looked worn down, but they were still so kind. Tender. He held her hand on the outside of his face.

"Why, Daddy?" Her voice was quiet.

"I don't know," he mouthed back, barely making a sound.

"You could have called me. I thought you were cutting me out of your life."

"I'd never do that. I just made such a bad mess of things I didn't know how to tell you."

Mingus's eyes started to tear.

"We made a pact, Daddy. We were always supposed to tell each other the truth with no exceptions. This was so unfair. I had to listen to Eva and M'Dea and wonder if everything they were saying was true. It *was* true. But part of me didn't believe it because I didn't hear it from you."

All he could do was shake his hand. Mingus felt so sorry for her father, for him not knowing he could account on her.

"I'm going to tell you this now, Daddy, before you hear it from someone else. I offered to be M'Dea's lawyer against you. She turned me down, but I didn't know what else to do. She's my mom and I wanted to help her and that's the only thing I had to offer."

He hugged her. They stayed like that. Standing in the aisle, not wanting to let go.

"You don't have to apologize to me, Mingus, I should have never put you in this situation."

She wiped her eyes.

"I just feel like I betrayed you."

"Look at me." He lifted her chin with his hand. "I'm your daddy, if no one else in this entire world knows your heart, I know your heart."

They walked into his office, the size of a large walk-in closet, and shut the door behind them. They sat facing each other. He held Mingus's hand between the two of his. His palms were the color of coffee creamer with cinnamon lines dissecting the calloused surfaces. He was still her first friend. The one who taught her how to fish and laid cement in the backyard for her tetherball court. Played hopscotch with her on lop-sided squares drawn in yellow construction chalk. Let her sit on his lap as he drove and turn the steering wheel. He'd spent time with her, quality time, even when Eva didn't want to and M'Dea was busy around the house. Mingus squeezed his hand and wondered how she could have forgotten those things.

Right then and there she decided. It did matter what he said. It didn't matter why. She loved him and nothing was going to change that. Mingus realized she hadn't come there for M'Dea or anyone else. She'd come for herself. To make sure their bond was still intact. The drama between he and M'Dea had nothing to do with her. Their history couldn't be broken by anything—family or otherwise.

Chapter 28

I thought it would stop if I slept with the lights on. I even sprinkled dried sage in my pillowcase. Carl's Mom used to put sage leaves under my pillow every night for the first year I lived in her house. Said it would stop the dreams and help me sleep peacefully. It started to work after a while, as soon as I started believing in it. Maybe that was the problem, I had stopped believing. Or maybe I just needed fresh sage instead of the dried stuff from my seasoning rack.

I was soaking wet and afraid to move from under the blankets. My pink nylon gown stuck to my skin. The sheets were damp and cold. The nightmare seemed worse when I slept in our bed. I woke up screaming: *You can't take my baby, you can't take my baby!* Carl was standing over me this time, last time it was my father. Both of them had six-feet-long tentacles for arms. I refused to let go of my stomach and their arms wrapped around me like python bodies trying to squeeze my baby out of me. Both times I got away and ended up in a hospital bed giving birth. The first time I gave birth to Eva. The second time I gave birth to Sarah.

Chapter 29

August 14

Sometimes you just have to laugh. Not because it's funny, just because you saw it coming and kept smiling as it pulled you under.

She should have known. If not by the fact that it took Eva twenty-five years to bring it back, then by the fact that she was reading Scripture when Eva knocked. It was a weekend when Eric had gone fishing and she'd woken up in bed alone. She had gotten accustomed to waking up with Eric in her bed, sunlight catching their faces as they read the newspaper or talked about past loves like old friends.

Mingus sat on the bathroom floor with a drawer of miscellaneous items between her legs. That's where she found the Bible, underneath combs, ribbons, ponytail holders. She didn't recall how it had gotten there. It had been a while since she thought she needed it. The Bible was reserved for really bad times. Times when no one else was home or she was too embarrassed to tell a real person what had happened. God would listen impartially and keep it to himself. Even if she only talked to him on occasion.

She felt sacrilegious. Stuffing God under a jar of Blue Magic and hair-filled brushes. Mingus wiped the oil from the burgundy leather-bound cover with tissue and opened it. *Oh king, have I done hurt?* She closed it and flipped it back open. *For we know that if our earthly house of this tabernacle were dissolved, we have a building of God, a house not made with hands.* One more time for good measure, she closed and opened. *VERILY, VERILY, I say unto you, He that entereth not by the door into the sheepfold, but climbeth up some other way, the same is a thief and a robber.* The doorbell rang. Mingus folded the page.

"Just a second," she said, grabbing a beige tank top off a basket of unfolded laundry in the hallway. She slipped the tank over her black sports bra on the way to the door.

"Why you taking so long?"

Mingus didn't have to look through the peephole; she knew that voice backward.

"What, you got company?" Eva looked from under her yellow baseball cap at Mingus and brushed past her with a cardboard box the size of two shoe boxes in her hands.

"No," Mingus said, closing the door.

Eva placed the box on the living room table.

"Damn, you feeling free today. Your house always look this nasty?"

"Don't come over unannounced and try to nitpick, Eva. It's my cleaning day."

"Well, you gotta do every room at once?"

"That's how I do it."

Mingus sat down on the couch, fighting the urge to straighten the pile of disheveled papers at her feet. She wasn't sure why Eva had come, but she knew she'd have to wait until Eva was good and ready to announce the reason to find out. Mingus tucked her blue sock-covered feet under her thighs and bent at the waist to sort the papers on the floor.

"You ain't gonna ask what's in the box?"

Eva anchored her hand above her hip bone and shifted her weight onto her right leg.

Mingus looked up. Eva's eyes were shadowed by the bill of the cap. "Should I?"

"You just really know how to mess up a nigga's program." Eva rolled her shadowed eyes toward the ceiling and took a deep breath. "Anyway," she said, fumbling the crisscrossed flaps on the box, "I wanted you to have this—have it back really. That's why I didn't wrap it, it belongs to you. I found this box by a trash Dumpster—anyway, here."

Mingus sat still for a moment then slowly unfolded her legs from under her lap and stood up. The chances were fifty-fifty it was something bad. She uncrossed the brown corrugated flaps. Under about a dozen newspaper balls was a patchwork dress with black patent leather lace-up boots. A shiny brown porcelain face. Curly black hair. Mingus took it out of the box.

"Marilyn."

"Yeah, I thought you'd remember."

Mingus sat back down on the edge of the couch. She held the doll in her arms as if it were a real baby. Head supported by her lower arm. Body pulled close to her chest.

"Where did you find this?"

"I stole it," Eva said.

Mingus didn't want to hear any more. Eva had brought it back. That had to mean something. She looked down at the doll's thin red-painted lips. She remembered Eva with two ribboned ponytails on her head, walking into the living room with Miss Marilyn's body dragging on the carpet as she clutched one arm in her fist. Eva wanted to take the doll to school with her for show-and-tell. Said that all her classmates had white dolls and she wanted to take Marilyn in.

Eva had all white dolls too. Mingus knew that Eva would feel special being the only kid at show-and-tell with a black doll. But how many times had Eva been mean to Mingus or closed her bedroom door in her face. Mingus told her no. Said it was her doll and that Eva couldn't even play with it. Eva flung the doll at Mingus and told her to take the funky thing. Mingus did. Placed it back on her bed. The next morning it was missing, only Mingus didn't notice. M'Dea got her up for school like normal. It wasn't until that night when she reached for the doll in her sleep that she realized it was gone.

Eva had taken the doll to show-and-tell anyway. Told M'Dea someone had stole it from her desk at recess.

"You want cranberry juice?"

Mingus propped the doll on the couch and walked toward the kitchen.

"That shit's nasty."

"All I have besides water."

"Then give me a lotta ice so I can't taste it. Don't you have no air-condition?"

Mingus didn't answer. Just poured two glasses of cranberry juice to their rims. One with no ice, the other with two cubes. She wondered how Eva could hide that doll for all those years and never mention it. Mingus walked back into the living room with the two glasses in her hands. Eva had made her way to the loveseat.

"Thanks for bringing back the doll; how's the job going?"

"So far pretty cool. What I want to know is, what's up with you and Eric?"

Mingus fought the impulse to smile. Behind a long sip of cranberry juice she stilled the giddiness she felt before she started to speak.

"What do you mean?" she said.

"Shit, the brothah's got it goin' on. That's what I mean. Y'all friends or y'all fucking?"

"Why does everything have to be about sex?"

" 'Cause sex is important. You can be out a lotta things, but if you gotta bald head and a hard dick, you're all right."

Mingus had to sip to that one. "A bald head, huh." She thought about the first time they were together and how Eric had opened her like a ripe pomegranate with the rhythm of his head. She could have sworn she'd fallen in love that night.

"Yeah, y'all doing it, 'cause you're trying to be too secretive."

"I'm not being secretive, Eva."

"Why ain't you answered my question then?"

Eva licked the rim of her glass.

" 'Cause you're nosey and nasty, that's why."

Eva smacked her lips.

"M'Dea already spilt it. Told me about Eric *and* the white boy." Eva clapped her hands and stomped her sandaled feet into the floor. "Mingus is trying to be a player. Go player! Go player! It's your birthday!"

Mingus shook her head.

"You're really sick, you know that, right? I only mentioned that to M'Dea in passing. Our conversation was about something completely different."

"I'm not blaming you. Some people need two, three dicks to be happy. Where's the Latin one at?" Eva stuck out her hand like she was waiting for Mingus to hand it over.

"You are trifling and Steven and I are just friends. We've caught a few bites to eat, but that's it."

"Um hum. I've had a friend or two myself. You ain't got to justify nothing to me. This ain't none of my business."

Mingus leaned back into the couch and sat the doll on her lap.

"Did you hate me when we were younger?" Mingus said.

"Why do you always have to spoil the mood? That's why I can't ever spend any time with you. You're too damned serious."

"Why can't you just answer the question? I won't get mad; I just want to know why you were always so mean to me."

Eva popped up.

"I'm going. My car still isn't ready and I have to catch the bus back."

"You want a ride?"

"Nope, I'd rather take the bus."

"Well, Daddy told me to tell you hello, by the way. And that he loves you."

"You be sure to tell him I didn't reciprocate."

Eva left. Mingus sat on the couch with Marilyn until the hurting stopped.

Chapter 30

I didn't take those divorce papers. Left them right there on the table where she had put them. Jumped in my car and drove a straight line to Glenda's house. Wasn't no one else I could turn to after a fight with my wife but Glenda. She knew how to patch me back together again. Especially after a fight with Ellie.

I didn't know how she was going to take this one, me leaving the divorce papers on the table. She's been waiting for this divorce for a long time. Me too, in a way. Waiting for something I never thought was going to come.

Ellie surprised me. Actually made me smile, thinking about the gumption she had in her. Withdrawing $40,000 of my hard-earned money from the bank. Picking up that car. Giving Glenda a good piece of her mind. Serving the divorce papers. Wasn't nothing funny about them divorce papers, but the whole day left me wishing she could let her hair down more regular. She sounded more like Glenda than herself. Her first all balled up, the fire eyes, made me feel something for her I ain't felt in a long time. I respected her again. Maybe for the first time. She was standing up for herself. And even though she was standing up against me, it felt all right.

I parked my car in front of the house and started across the grass. Walked up the five cement steps to the door. Seemed like I got tired all of a sudden, like my knees were gonna cut out from under me.

"Baby, you look wiped out. Come here and grab a seat." Glenda massaged my shoulders. Knew how to press her thumbs into the tight spaces and work out the kinks. "Yeah, that's better already, want me to fix you a drink?"

"A taste of Black Velvet, no ice, would be good."

"You see this here?" She pointed to a glass on the table. "Black Velvet, no ice. Figured you was gonna need one; I fixed it as you parked."

I liked that about Glenda. How she anticipated my need and handled it, whatever it was.

Glenda was a down home woman despite the fact she was from California. Her spirit made me feel comfortable. Wasn't much pretense about her. She wore a short dusky brown afro and made most of her jewelry out of beads and other little knickknacks she'd come across. She was natural, what I thought a woman should be. No makeup, hospitable, a lot of meat on her bones. She made me feel safe.

And Glenda was a hustler like a dice man on a Chicago street corner. Could run up toe to toe with any ole body. I liked that. Knew I didn't have to worry about her much.

I stared over at Glenda and noticed she had on those jeans I liked so much. She sat with her toes tucked under the middle cushion of the sofa watching *Jeopardy*.

"You look good," I told her.

"Feels good to come home and take off that clown suit and wig. It's a shame we always have to fit some Eurocentric archetype to be accepted. If people's minds weren't so messed up, black people's minds included, I would be able to go to work in these jeans and a natural, even a galee, and it wouldn't make a bit of difference. But shit don't run that way, do it?" She laughed. "Nope.

And I ain't crying about it. How you doing? Looking all lost over there."

"Coulda thought of better ways to spend my afternoon. Had some properties I wanted to look at today."

"That woman is out of control, I tell you." Glenda snapped her neck. "She came to my *job,* Carl—probably trying to get me fired. One day I'm going to thank her for it though. All this is only going to make us stronger. White bitch."

I cringed. Somewhere in my soul I cringed. That word sounded so opposite of anything Ellie was.

"And she's sneaky. Not only did she sneak herself down there to buy a car, she tried to trick me into talking about my personal life. Talking 'bout a person should know something about the people they do business with—if you want it, buy it; if you don't, don't waste my time. You don't need to know shit about me; I ain't going home with your ass."

Glenda reached over to the coffee table and grabbed her toe-nail file. I took a few more sips of my drink and tried to relax myself.

"When I finally figured out who she was, I was outdone. You hear me? Outmothafuckindone. You never told me she was white, Carl. And it's not like you never mentioned her either. Ellie this, Ellie that. You just decided to leave that part out, huh? Describing that woman as light-skinned. Light-skinned, my ass, white is what you should have been saying. Uh uh, ain't no need in explaining now, save it. Talking to her one minute I could see she was just a run-of-the-mill white girl, what black man wouldn't want to keep her a secret."

Glenda switched from her toes to her fingernails.

"And evil, Carl, I'm telling you, that woman ain't nothing nice. Only description I can think of is evil. Plain-assed evil red-headed bitch."

"Okay baby, that's enough. You done talked bad about the woman enough."

"You ain't heard the half of it. Trying to get my commission taken away after I worked with her all morning. I shoulda really let her know why she lost her husband."

"Enough, Glenda."

"*Enough?* How many times have I listened to you talk bad about that woman? Now you gonna sit up here and tell me *enough?* You defending her now?"

I stuck my glass back up to my mouth. I didn't wanna hurt Glenda, she was a good woman, but she wasn't 'bout to say another bad word against Ellie.

"Defending your wife, ain't that about a bitch? What, you trying to sneak through the back door now?"

"Glenda, I ain't trying to do nothin'. Just ain't no reason for you to talk about her any kinda way."

"You're about to fuck up, Carl."

"What? Don't curse me, woman."

"You're turning soft. Now that the ball's rolling, you're trying to get sentimental."

"You expect I have no feelings for her because we're getting divorced?"

"You should have thought about that shit before you got involved in something else. Now I'm tied up."

"I told you my situation first day you met my black ass."

"You told me you weren't happy, that you were ready to leave your relationship. You changing your mind now?"

"Glenda, quit putting words in my mouth. All I'm saying is don't disrespect my wife."

"*Your wife.* Today she's your wife, huh? What was she yesterday when you were sleeping in my bed and eating dinner with my children?"

"My wife."

"Mothafuckinsonofabitch. You talk all this game about leaving her but that don't mean nothing, does it? I ain't seen paper number one and it's been almost two years of this shit."

"She filed."

"And when was this?"

"I don't know. She gave me the papers today."

"That's what this is. You're in your mourning stage. Probably thinking you want to go back to that bitch. Let me tell you something. Divorce ain't going to put your shit back together again."

"I asked you not to call her outside of her name."

"What, *bitch?* Is that what you're talking about? She is a no-count, greasy-haired, white trailer-trash bitch and ain't a damn thing you can do to change it."

"What does that make you?"

"You probably think I'm one, but does it matter? I'm not the one who's married."

I got up. Slammed my glass down on the end table and headed to the closet at the end of the hall. I grabbed the few jackets and slacks I had hung up and put them over my arm. Reached down and grabbed my two pair of dress shoes, then walked back into the living room.

Glenda was crying. Her arms wrapped around her knees. Her face looking all broken up.

"What am I supposed to tell Ty and Sarah?" she said.

"Anything I left, you can throw away. I won't be back."

"You can't do this, Carl, it isn't right."

"Tell the kids I love them or don't tell them; I don't want to confuse them right now."

"I believed you," she said, making my heart drop, "I believed we were going to be together. You lied."

"Goodbye, Glenda."

I threw my things in the trunk. I just drove, catching speed, not wanting to stop. The windows rolled up tight, I tried to hear my inner voice above all the racket in my head. What am I, I thought. If Glenda was a bitch, what did that make me?

Chapter 31

August 20
I asked Eric why he'd never gotten married.
He said most women don't want a healthy black
man. I was speechless.

He touched her like she was delicate. Not nervously, but in a strumming fashion. Like he knew her strings had been broken before. He mended her. And she relinquished fully each hurt. He moved over her with attention in his fingers, in his lips. Her breasts blossomed under his tongue. Her thighs relaxed into him. Mingus closed her eyes and drifted in the gentleness of his rhythm.

The movement was thick, but slow. They tarried in each other, gaining momentum with the deepness of breath. This was the first time she liked it with the lights on. She wanted to be seen by him. She trusted him; and as he cupped her face in his hands, she let her tears flow freely into his palms. She was beautiful in this moment.

"You ever think about kids," he said softly into her ear.

She nodded yes into his shoulder.

Eric groped the hair at the nape of her neck and kissed around her jawline.

"I want a basketball starting lineup," he said.

"So do I," Mingus said, never having thought about so many children before, only wanting what he wanted. "So do I."

Chapter 32

I had some photo albums in the family room, but most of the pictures were between Mingus's old closet and the garage. I found myself making a day of sitting in the garage with the door flipped up looking through old boxes. Boxes and trunks I hadn't looked through in years.

One of the boxes was so old, the adhesive tape had jelled yellow and crinkled into itself. I tore off the tape and found my graduation dress. Graduation-dress-slash-wedding-gown. It wasn't eggshell white anymore. Actually it looked more gray or dusty beige. It looked so tiny. Tiny like the little girl who wore it as her wedding gown couldn't have known what she was doing. I remember so clearly picking out that pattern with my mama. The two of us walking from fabric store to fabric store deciding which cloth would go best.

I thought I was grown back then. That that dress was going to mark the coming-out of a woman. My mama was so proud. She spent every penny of her sock money on the materials. My father said I could graduate in jeans for all he cared. Mama told me in secret that he was being foolish. That I was the first Shannon-O'Brien to graduate in thirty years. The very first to graduate in the United States. Said that my family had worked the land and that I would do better than that. I thought I would too. I mean, I really thought so. And my mama worked so hard on that dress. Putting it together with double stitches and no sewing machine.

I wish there was some way I could have told her it was going to be my wedding dress. Somehow she would have made it even more special. Maybe added Victorian lace trim. Maybe just wished on it for me. That my husband would be good to me and love me for always and forever. Mama could have done that had she known. But I didn't even know. I just wanted to graduate and get a steady occupation. Get a small living space so I could feel at peace with myself. So I wouldn't have to listen to my father talk drunken nonsense and keep my mother up all night. I wasn't really asking or wanting all that much. Just some sacred, quiet space.

Carl was frosting on top. Everything opposite of what my dad said a black man was supposed to be. Clean. Intelligent. Called me miss. Hadn't anyone called me miss around my hometown before. I was just plain old Ellie O'Brien. Lem's daughter. I had an identity with Carl. An identity all my own that I defined myself each minute I dealt with him. He respected me as a woman, not as a child, not as Lem's daughter. As me. Me meant something with him.

I trailed back into the house with two armloads of photo albums. The old silk covers had turned from bright to pale. Pale roses, pale leaves. But I was looking for pictures. Pictures of Eva and Mingus when they were babies. Any of Carl as a child if I could find them.

I looked through sixteen albums, peeled back the brittle plastic flaps, and took out thirty-four pictures. I took my stack and one by one laid each picture flat on the coffee table. The girls looked so cute. Curly-haired combinations of me and Carl. I used to want to take them home to my father and let him see how wrong he was. Let him see that white and black did mix, perfectly, into two beautiful little girls.

I had always wanted more children. I imagined myself with a full house of them. Three rooms. Two, three children to each room. I imagined big meals and a whole bunch of laughter. Always someone in the house. Always someone on the phone or in the bathroom. I would have been Big Mama, maybe even Grandma M'Dea by now. But Carl said that two was more than enough. That with two you could travel and still get out of the house. We never got out of the house. And even back then I knew that home was where my place was. Maybe even farther back than I let on to.

I settled into motherhood smoothly. Despite the subtle resentments Carl never discussed with me. The ones that made him sleep on the couch some nights or fall asleep next to me fully clothed. His mother used to tell me that the mistrust would pass. After he got used to the fact that he was married. She said that no man likes to feel trapped. Even if he helped throw the net himself. I never felt trapped. I felt saved. Like Carl had come along and picked me up out of a life I couldn't have escaped from by myself. I was thankful to him. He gave me Eva, the first person besides my mother who ever loved me unconditionally.

I knew the condom was old. I didn't know where it had come from, but even still I could tell it was old. I had found it in the street when I was sixteen. Package was all beat up. I kept it. Buried it under a eucalyptus in my schoolyard. Checked there almost every day for two years. I'd sit under the tree with my packed lunch. Sit cozy between two thick exposed roots and use Mama's metal spoon to dig up my shallow treasure. I knew that I'd use it one day.

That's the part of me that says I knew what I was doing. That with all my good intentions, I still had sex with him knowing the condom would break. That's why I unwrapped it myself. That's why I didn't let him see the worn-down package or let him slip it on. I let him slip into me, despite the sinking feeling of dishonesty in my heart. And unlike him, I did hear it pop. If not physically, then in my heart I heard it.

He was my first, I wanted him to be my forever.

I'd kept my silence and it had cost me. Now I wondered if he was keeping his. I needed those old pictures to figure out the truth. I needed to know if Carl had brought another life into this world. The life I had given birth to in my dream.

Chapter 33

November 19

I saw Eva's ex-man in the mall food court. I was catching some lunch before returning to the office. He thought I knew that Eva got fired for coming into work drunk after a three-month probation. I didn't.

They were lying in bed the night Mingus found out Eva had been spreading her business. Eric lay lengthwise and Mingus crossed his body like a T, her head sinking ever so slightly into his stomach.

"I can't believe you," Mingus said, popping a kernel of popcorn into her mouth. "You have talked so much trash about meeting me while I was on a date with a white man, now I find out that you sexed half the white female population at your university?"

"A couple."

"More than three?"

"Basically."

Mingus turned onto her stomach and faced him.

"When were you going to tell me this?"

"I wasn't," he said, a devilish grin spreading on his lips.

"You know that's a double standard, right? I don't ever want to hear another word from you about Steven."

"You were dating," Eric said.

Mingus rolled her eyes.

"Please. Don't tell me you're one of those black men who thinks fucking and dating are different."

"They are, aren't they?" Eric smoothed his hand over his goatee and adjusted his head in the pillow. "I sexed a couple, you were looking for a husband."

"I never had sex with Steven, so whose relationships went deeper? And I'm mixed, how does that twist it?"

"Damn near every black person in America is mixed. And every last one of them have the same story: *My great-great-grandfather on my half-dead uncle's side of the family was a quarter Cherokee and on my mama's side—*"

She hit his shoulder.

"That's not funny, Eric, you know my mom's white."

He kissed her forehead.

"And you're black."

He kissed her again.

Mingus had always felt more black than white. But there was something about what Eric said that unnerved her. Like he was denying that a part of her existed. The same part that she had denied many times herself.

"I am black, but I'm also part white, you can't just act like I am not. And I don't like your little half-dead uncle joke either."

"I'm sorry, baby, but don't get so bent out of shape. You must admit the mixed biracial thing is pretty popular right now. Everybody's talking about how they're mixed with this or that."

"Well, being biracial in the seventies wasn't trendy. It was hard. And it still is hard. So anyone who minimizes what a person goes through, doesn't know."

He took her hand in his.

"I apologize again. And I'm not denying your whiteness. You are what you are; I can't change that."

"Would you change it if you could?"

Mingus looked him in the eye.

"Baby, you are really tripping. I like you and want you just as you are. How did we get into this anyway?"

"We were talking about whose interracial relationships went deeper, yours or mine."

"Well, I guess we know the answer to that."

"Yours," she said.

"We are going to end up arguing if we keep this up. All I have to say is this—sex is a private act that takes place behind closed doors with no witnesses. It's a lot different than going out in public to dinners and lunches like you were doing."

"You ain't nothing nice," Mingus said, giving him a disdainful look. Behind the look, she realized she was caught. She'd never told Eric about the lunches. Only two people knew: M'Dea and Eva.

Mingus lay there with her eyes closed, slowly chewing a kernel of popcorn. The uneasiness of conviction turned in her stomach.

"I have something to tell you." Mingus sat up Indian-style facing Eric. "When we first started dating," she took a deep breath, "in our first couple of weeks, I kissed Steven."

"Just kissed?" Eric asked.

Mingus shook her head no.

"We didn't have sex. We didn't even come close to having sex. I made out with him though."

"Really?" Eric said after a long pause.

"I know I shouldn't have, I'm not making excuses for myself, I just really needed to let you know."

"Why did you?"

Mingus wrung her hands in her lap.

"I was scared. I really liked you. Last time I really liked someone he took me for a loop and left me midrelationship. I was trying to protect myself."

"You thought I was going to be a chump, in other words."

"My instincts told me you weren't, but look where my instincts have gotten me in the past."

"I see."

"Look, Eric, you don't have to be nice to me. I know you probably want to scream at me. Leave me maybe. You don't have to stay here; I understand."

"That was wrong, Mingus; I asked you on at least three occasions if you were interested in a relationship with him."

"I'm sorry."

Mingus covered her eyes, partly so he wouldn't see her cry, partly so she wouldn't have to watch him get dressed and walk away.

"I'm not leaving you." He pulled her hands from her eyes. "I don't like this, but I'm not going to leave you over it."

Maybe this was what she needed to believe in him. For her to mess up and him to still be there, still want to be there. She felt like this time she was in love with someone who knew how to handle it.

"Come here," he said, patting his chest, motioning for her to lay against him. He tipped her chin up so that he stared directly into her eyes. "You do understand that I wouldn't be comfortable with you seeing him anymore, don't you?"

Mingus nodded her head then closed her eyes.

"Who told you about the lunches?"

"Mingus—"

"It's not important, I just need to hear it."

"Don't get mad at her. We were just talking about you one day and she mentioned it randomly. I really didn't think much of it."

"She was talking out of context, you know that, right?" Mingus kept her head on his chest. "The making out thing happened one time, that's all. It makes me mad that she would interfere in our relationship like that. I'm gonna talk to her about it."

"Don't even trip, Mingus. She's probably just lonely."

"I don't care what her problem is, it's not right."

"Why don't you invite her to our dinner Saturday night."

Mingus looked at Eric like he was out of his cotton-picking mind.

"Why the hell would I do that? Last thing I want is to meet your parents and have my sister tripping on me at the same time."

"She's probably jealous, Mingus, you have to understand that. She has this handsome boss who happens to be fawning over her younger sister. Probably damages her ego. Invite her and we can introduce her to my brother Brandon. I think they'd hit it off."

"If she didn't go with me over to our mother's on her anniversary, I doubt if she'd come to this."

"Just ask the girl," Eric said.

Mingus thought about it. Maybe Eva did need some male energy to balance her out. Maybe she and Brandon would click. Still, she wasn't sure.

"Okay, Eric, but if this thing goes bad or your parents end up hating me, you know who I'm blaming for it."

Chapter 34

I know now that there are levels of sin. The sin I committed against my mother by not telling her about Carl before I ran off, never saying goodbye to her. Not telling Carl that the condom was old and could break. All those things considered, I should have never found out about a baby from a videotape. If I had never heard another piece of truth uttered from his mouth, I should have heard this.

The end hit me. I had known it was coming, but I felt different once it arrived. The I-nevers cemented themselves into me. He would never leave his toothbrush on the edge of the sink again. I would never fix him another bowl of soup or oatmeal with dollops of cinnamon and brown sugar. We would never disrobe and touch intimate spaces thirty-five years caused us to memorize. There would be no thirty-six.

He had left me hanging on, and he had let go. The rejection of being put away fostered a tender hate inside of me. I figured out that bitterness sits behind eyes that can't cry. I resented him for the person I had regressed into. For the seven hundred and seventy-four ticks of celibacy in the back of my checkbook. For the two years and forty-three days I lay in bed untouched. I had filed my dreams of more children away years ago. I just hoped for his love in our older age. He gave both to someone else.

I had lined the pictures up on the coffee table. Fifteen pictures of Eva, eighteen of Mingus, one of Carl as a three-year-old sitting on his mother's skirted lap trying to bite into the skin of an apple. I studied carefully each of the pictures. The curve of their noses. How Mingus's and Eva's were both smaller versions of Carl's. Eva's slightly more pointed, all three having short, flat bridges that flared into full, perfectly rounded nostrils. Mingus and Carl having matching brown moles that sat just outside the crease of the left nostril. And then there was the space between the eyes, how their eyebrows tipped inward when they smiled and their bottom lips almost completely disappeared against their teeth.

I stared hard at these pictures. And all of a sudden it felt like Carl had had the girls by himself. They didn't look like me. They didn't have my eyes, my skin tone, my smile. I felt crushed twice. Because as I looked at the videotape, replayed it and paused it on Sarah, I saw her in them. I saw that she had their eyes and the curve of their noses. The mole against her left nostril. I knew in a matter of seconds that she was his. And in that same second, Eva and Mingus were less mine. Because before I had seen myself in them. And wherever that space had been, I couldn't find it any-more. Carl had taken that away from me, along with everything else.

Chapter 35

November 23

*I've never looked so forward to holidays in my
life. Christmas in love, it almost feels like
I've never had one. Eric said he was going to
change all that. I can already see an eight-foot
Douglas fir in my living room window. Eric
and me stringing the lights, hanging our
special ornament that says Eric's and
Mingus's first Christmas. I can see it.
Almost like it's already happened.*

She got that sinking feeling. Like her life force was being drained from her womb. Like she was on her period. Only she wasn't. Everything was fine. She was seated with Eric and his family. Eric at one end of the table, his stepfather at the other. Every once in a while Eric's mom would ask Mingus a question, then squeeze her hand hard if she liked her answer. Everything was going well. Except for one thing. Next to Eric's brother Brandon was an empty seat. An empty seat Mingus expected full well would be filled before the end of the evening.

Both Mingus and Eric got up from the table to serve the food. Mingus carried a homemade stuffing, green beans with pearl onions, and sliced red potatoes. Eric carried the carved deep-fried turkey and whole cranberry sauce. They were just about to hold hands for grace when the doorbell rang. Eric placed his napkin next to his plate and went to the door.

She was straight out of a music video. Red lipstick, red heels, and a red crushed velvet minidress with spaghetti straps. She must have been almost five-seven with those four-inch stiletto heels on. Mingus liked her new haircut, layered oil-slicked curls tapered on the sides, slightly faded in the back. She must be late because of the hair, Mingus thought. She watched her sister walk down three small steps into the dining room. Mingus was convinced that no woman with that much behind should wear a dress that short in public.

Eric extended one arm out to the seated crowd and placed the other arm around Eva, squeezing her waist.

"Everyone, this is Eva, Mingus's sister. This here is my mother Clairice, my father Chuck, my brother Brandon. Of course you know Mingus."

"Pleased to meet all of you." Eva smiled teasingly, like a movie star to her fans.

Mingus dropped her napkin to her plate and walked over to the two of them.

"Would you like something to drink?" she said to Eva.

Eva looked directly at Eric. "What do you have?"

"What would you like?" Mingus breathed into her face.

"I'll pass for now," Eva said, leaving Eric's side. She walked to her seat next to Brandon.

Rude. Mingus's eyes followed Eva to her seat. "Anyone need a refill?"

"Everyone's fine, baby," Eric said. "I think we should pray for the food."

"I think we forgot a few of the things in the kitchen."

Mingus turned and walked toward the kitchen. Eric paused

momentarily then followed. Mingus waited for Eric to cross the threshold then slid the door closed.

"What was that, Eric?" she whispered, looking him dead in the eye, her chest slightly brushing against his.

"What was what?"

"Putting your hands around her waist. Are you attracted to that slutty shit?"

Eric stepped back.

"Slow your horses, Mingus, you're overreacting to nothing. All I did was introduce your sister."

"Let you tell it."

"What are you saying, I'm attracted to your sister?" Eric cocked his head and looked hard at Mingus. "I'm the one who wanted her to meet my brother, remember?"

"There was no reason for you to leave your hand around her waist that long, Eric. There was no reason for you to put your hand there in the first place."

"I would introduce any woman I know that way, including you."

"Hold up," Mingus said, sticking out her hand halt style. "I'm your woman supposedly and you *didn't* introduce me that way tonight. And furthermore, I didn't even get formally introduced to your mother. Eva's ass did."

"Oh, you're *supposedly* my woman?" Eric lowered his voice, but his face gained intensity. "You have the damn keys to my house and you're supposedly my woman now?"

Mingus ignored him.

"Matter of fact, now that I think about it, Eric, you didn't even introduce me to your family; I introduced myself."

"Ming, this situation has been blown completely out of proportion."

"Don't call me Ming. I'm serious, Eric, I'm not comfortable with this. You were squeezing her waist and she was squeezing you back. Is that what you guys do around the studio all day? Squeeze on each other in the editing bays?"

"Baby, you are trippin' a little too hard." Eric held her arms above the elbows and pushed her gently against the counter. "I love you, I'm in love with you—not your sister. I want you. You are the only woman I want in my bed, in my life. The way I'm thinking, I want you to be my wife someday. I'm not bullshitting. So don't let this peripheral shit cloud your vision, okay? Even if your sister did have a little crush on me, nothing can shake me from you."

"You think she has a crush on you? Maybe her working with you isn't a good idea after all."

"No, baby, and it wouldn't matter if she did."

He kissed around her face. He had said all the right words. The right intonations, the right assuring gazes.

"You've never told me that before."

"What?" he said.

"That you love me."

"I'm in love with you, woman, okay?" He pressed her chin up to his lips. "You're the best thing that ever happened to me. Even my family knows it. The main reason I invited them here was to meet you. You understand what I'm talking about?"

"Yeah," she said softly, embarrassed she'd been tripping so hard. "I just don't want anything to happen to us, Eric."

"Baby, we got that thang going on, nothing can touch us."

"You sure?"

"Listen. I, ERIC JAMES SIMMS, LOVE MINGUS JANAY BROWNING WITH ALL OF MY HEART. Is that loud enough for you, you need me to say it louder?"

"No," Mingus said giggling. She grabbed both of his hands. "You forgive me, baby?"

"You know, doubting me is gonna cost you."

"Name it."

Eric's expression changed from playful to serious.

"Promise me fourteen thousand and five morning kisses."

"Is that it?"

He nodded and kissed her lips.

"That one didn't count."

They reentered the dining room, Mingus with prairie rolls in her hand, Eric with a sweet potato pie. They placed both dishes at the end of the table.

"What was the commotion in there? Sounded like you were screaming."

"I was, Mama." He grabbed Mingus around the waist. "I was declaring my undying love for this woman so that she knows she's the only woman I need."

"Sounds like an insecurity problem to me," Eva mumbled into her half-empty glass. Mingus assumed Brandon had poured it for her.

"Shall we pray?"

Eric's stepfather led the prayer. *Bless us, O Lord, for these our gifts, that we are about to receive . . .* Mingus had never heard her father lead grace. He never even sat at the head of the table. If there was just the four of them, the head chairs stayed empty. If there was company, the guest was given the head chair. He used to say that he headed up too many other things and didn't need extra pressure. Mingus thought about the fact that M'Dea always carved the turkey. Maybe her father knew way back then that he belonged to another family. That one day he'd be carving turkey in *their* house.

"Now, Mingus," Clairice said, spooning cranberry sauce onto her plate, "you expect me to believe that my son, who has never prepared an edible meal in his life, cooked all of this food for us?"

"Cooked, chopped, and seasoned. I just gave him a few recipes and cooking hints."

"An old dog can learn new tricks if he has the right woman at his side," Brandon said, cocking his head toward Eva.

Eva giggled, acting coquettish—wasn't a thing shy about her, Mingus thought. Eric's mother glanced in Eva's direction, then turned her gaze back to Mingus.

"So you practice law."

"Yes."

"Estate planning, is it?"

"Yes." Mingus chewed the last of the stuffing in her mouth. "I started out doing litigation for an insurance company then moved into this area."

"How long have you practiced?"

"Almost six years now."

"At twenty-nine, very impressive."

"Twenty-nine, but I'll be thirty in less than a month."

"Don't forget to tell her how you graduated a whole year early." Eva bit into a prairie roll. Mingus pretended she hadn't heard her.

"A year early." Clairice squeezed Mingus's hand and turned toward Eva. "What's your profession, young lady?"

"I'm a personal assistant. Eric's personal assistant."

"You work with my son?"

"Up close and personal, every day, five days a week."

Eva looked directly at Mingus as she spoke.

"Except for next week," Mingus squeezed Clairice's hand back. "Eric and I are taking a couple days off to spend with you and Chuck while you're visiting."

"Could you get me another one of these? No ice."

Eva slid her glass in Brandon's direction. Mingus could tell from Eva's expression she hadn't known about the time off.

"Dad, how's the house coming along?" Eric said, avoiding Eva's stare. "Mom told me you laid a new driveway."

"Yeah, Clairice and I decided to put in a circular drive. We can pull right up to the front door now if we want to."

"And by the time Brandon and you decide to give us grandchildren," Clairice said, glancing at both of her sons, "we'll probably have pulled up the backyard and put in a Jacuzzi or something."

"I'm practicing, Mama, I'm practicing," Brandon said, temporarily ceasing his side conversation with Eva.

"At least Eric is moving in the right direction. Mingus is a fine young woman. I haven't even seen a suitable prospect in your case. Gonna wait till you catch something then wish you would have settled down."

"Maybe this sweet thang in red will straighten me out."

Clairice puckered her lips to say something but stopped herself.

"What do you all think about interracial dating?" Eva chimed in out of the blue. "Maybe we should ask Mingus about that. Mingus?"

The tit for tat exchanges were becoming too much. "I think it's a personal choice. If the individuals are happy, other people should butt out."

"Well spoken, dear. Now Eric told me that your mother is Caucasian and your father is African American?"

"Yeah." Mingus cut her eyes at Eva. "My mother's family is Irish and my father was raised in Shreveport, Louisiana, until he was six."

"They met there?"

"No, they met in North Carolina while my father was stationed there."

"And they're still together, how wonderful."

Eva winked at Mingus, then coughed.

"Actually," Mingus said, "they're getting divorced."

"I'm sorry to hear that."

"Me too. Sometimes things just don't work out."

"And sometimes they do," Eva said.

Eva dropped her napkin to her plate and dusted off her lap.

"Don't start, Eva."

"I ain't startin'. Sometimes certain things were never meant to be in the first place and it takes time to figure that out."

"And sometimes certain people are so closed-minded they can't accept things beyond their control."

"Exactly."

The entire table was dumbfounded, including Mingus. She'd let Eva get to her in the presence of witnesses. I shouldn't have invited her, Mingus thought. She shouldn't have invited or worried about her selfish behind.

Eva plopped a cube of ice into her mouth.

"Okay." Eric held Mingus's hand. "Now that we've had entertainment, who wants dessert?"

Chapter 36

I wanted to name Eva Sarah, after Sassy Sarah Vaughan. Ellie said she would never name her child after that woman. Said over her dead body. I half remember the look on her face. We were sitting by ourselves in my mama's living room. Cozying up under each other on the couch. I cupped my ear to Ellie's stomach and felt Eva kick. All I said was "Sarah," didn't even get in the last name before Ellie pushed my head up with both hands and wrapped her arms around her stomach. I glanced at her and no sooner than I looked, I saw her face breaking up into tears, her eyes going sad. She said her child would be named after her mother and not even a rainy day in hell could change that.

That's when I realized maybe I had been playing Sassy too much. That Elaine had gotten jealous, maybe even angry. But some music just gives you insight into yourself. *Last night, when we were young, love was a star, a song unsung, life was so new, so real, so bright, ages ago, last night,* and *If we'd thought a bit of the end of it, when we started painting the town, we'd have been aware that our love affair was too hot not to cool down . . . it was just one of those things.* A woman should never get mad at a man for speaking the truth. And music ain't ever the enemy.

That's when I stopped playing music with words around Ellie. So that way she couldn't accuse me of nothing. But as far as I was concerned, the lack of words didn't make me no less guilty of listening to the same type of music. "Passions of a Man," "Moanin'," "Things Ain't What They Used to Be." That's when I really started getting into Charlie Mingus. To a musician, notes and words are interchangeable, at least to me. And actually there are some notes that words can never touch, but Ellie didn't understand that. At least not in the beginning. So when I asked if we could name our next daughter Mingus, all she asked was if Mingus was male or female. When I said male, she said yes.

Chapter 37

December 4

Eva didn't tell me she slept with Brandon. I found out anyway. Not from Eric, from his mother. She'd overheard Brandon spilling the details to Eric the next morning. After that, even though his parents slept downstairs, I wouldn't let Eric touch me the rest of their visit. If blood flows thicker than water, I didn't want to end up guilty by association.

Eva apologized again. This time for the spectacle on Thanksgiving. She said that one day she hoped to be as happy as Mingus and Eric looked. That she was tired of making bad decisions in her life. Mingus didn't know how serious Eva was until the tears started to fall. She hadn't seen Eva cry since they were kids. Just that one time. And Mingus was only five when it happened so she wasn't sure she remembered correctly. She knew Eva's appendix had burst. The whole family rushed her to the hospital. M'Dea would tell Eva she was going to be okay and in the same breath she was screaming at Carl to drive faster. Mingus sat in her corner of the back seat against the door, the hood of her faux-fur-lined coat hiding her secret stare. And even though it was after midnight and even though Eva was silent, Mingus, if she concentrated hard enough, could see water glisten down Eva's cheek.

The TV muted, they sat at opposite ends of the couch. Prolonged silence had grown into a form of comfort. Eva's feet were covered in the tip of Mingus's throw blanket, her head tilted slightly sideways. Mingus sat with her legs pulled to her chest, watching the soundless conversation of two people whose fake lives could never parallel her real one.

"Are you ever . . ." Eva said facing away from Mingus, "are you ever afraid of turning out like M'Dea?"

"What do you mean?" Mingus said in an equally low tone.

"Alone. And not wanting to be."

Mingus turned her head toward Eva.

"I haven't really thought about it like that."

She had thought about it. Almost every night since she found out about the affair. It didn't matter whether Eric was lying next to her or not. She realized she'd attained a certain peace in being alone. At least in loneliness she had nothing to lose and everything to wish for. Having what she wanted was a different kind of pressure. She had to hold on to it. Preserve it. Not mess it up. All that took way more energy than wishing.

"Sometimes," Eva said, turning toward Mingus, "sometimes I think it's already happened to me. Like I'm stuck in some pit I started digging a long time ago and it's so deep now no one can see me anymore. I'm inside yelling, 'I'm still here, I'm right here,' but nobody wants to hear me. I've tried so hard, Mingus. It's like I inherited the right to have a fucked-up life."

"Thinking that way can't be helping you."

"It's my birthright. M'Dea messed up Carl's life by getting pregnant. Carl messed up M'Dea's life by marrying her. And I was the catalyst in all of it. That's the energy I was born into, wouldn't it make sense that my life would turn out the same way?"

Mingus pulled her legs tighter into her chest.

"I don't know," Mingus said, turning back toward the television.

"It just makes sense to me. That one day I'll meet a man who doesn't love me back, get pregnant, and raise the child on my own. At least I have sense enough not to marry him like M'Dea did."

"Do you really hate him?"

"Carl?"

Mingus nodded.

"Yes. With everything I have I hate him." She spoke calmly. "But you want to know the sad truth?"

"What?"

"Mostly I hate you."

Mingus didn't flinch.

"I knew that. I've just kept asking you, hoping you would lie."

"One thing I'm not is a liar," Eva said.

"I know."

Eva stirred slowly.

"I'm going to head home."

"You can stay or I can give you a ride."

"I actually like the bus. It's the one place I always see people worse off than me." Eva smiled. "Sick, huh?"

Mingus nodded and pulled the blanket that was on Eva's feet onto her own.

Eva's eyes were caught somewhere between fire and disappointment. She stood a foot in front of Mingus and placed her purse strap on her shoulder. "And just so you know, I didn't sleep with Brandon. I didn't even let him kiss me. He tried."

"Thanks for finally answering my question, about why we've never been close."

"It's not your fault it's this way between us. It's not mine either, I don't think. I'd rather love you. But our family wasn't made that way."

Mingus's nose ran but she didn't wipe it.

"Maybe you're right," Mingus said.

Eva stopped at tne door.

"Enjoy yourself over Daddy's new woman's house. I'll be sure to tell Mama you're joining the enemy camp."

" 'Bye, Eva. Lock my door, please."

Her words echoed in Mingus's head long after she was gone. Mingus eyed the square piece of paper clipped to her dashboard. Directions to Glenda's house. She did feel like a traitor, but her father had sounded so excited when he invited her to come. He told her that she was gonna love Glenda. But how could she love the woman who helped her father break her heart. She hated her. The same way a child hates brussels sprouts or haircuts. Or how Eva hated her. As much as she didn't want to disappoint him, there was no magic cure this time. Kiss and make it better wasn't going to work.

Mingus turned right on Redvine Avenue, immediately seeing two packs of grade school boys huddled thirty yards ahead. One boy, about thirteen, grabbed the football out of the pothole near the center of the street and bodies dispersed to both sides of the curb. Mingus drove slowly, looking closely at the faces she passed. So many hues. So many varying shades of blackness she'd never seen in her neighborhood growing up. Her family was always the *different* family on the block. And depending on who was talking, *different* could at any time be replaced by strange, weird, mixed-up, or worse. Mingus wondered if her father felt more normal living there. If in a sea of all-black faces he tried to forget white existed.

The trees on the block had almost completely lost their leaves. There were no sidewalks on the street. Just graying winter lawns rolled out like dingy carpet in front of faded houses. Mingus walked along the curb with a potted Christmas cactus in her hand. She climbed the concrete steps and knocked gently on the glass outer door.

"You must be Mingus." A woman with a short afro and brown frosted lipstick smiled into her eyes.

"I'm here to see my father."

"Come in." The woman adjusted the baby on her hip and closed both doors behind them. "A cactus, how nice. I've never gotten one of these before."

Mingus looked her in the face but didn't say a word. There was no remorse in her eyes. Not even the tiniest bit of apology.

"Want me to take that from you?"

Glenda gently pulled the ceramic pot from Mingus's hand and sat it on a table next to a cherry wood kinara. On the coat rack, Mingus immediately noticed her father's green army trench with brown pockets hanging from the top rung.

"Well, Mingus, it's very good meeting you. I'm Glenda, this on my hip is Sarah, and this is Tyson." Glenda rested her free hand on the boy's skinny shoulder and nudged him forward.

"Hi, I'm Ty. Nobody calls me Tyson but you can if you want to. I don't like the name Tyson very much. Ty sounds better."

"Hush your mouth, boy," Glenda said, yanking the collar of his shirt. "May I take your coat?"

She wasn't taking anything else from Mingus.

"I'm here to see my father."

"Oh, he'll be back in a few minutes, he ran to the market to pick up some French bread for dinner. Your father said you love pasta."

Mingus nodded slowly, counteracting Glenda's hyperactive tone.

"He also said you like shrimp. I cooked some of that too; I marinated it in crushed garlic and olive oil and baked it in seasoned bread crumbs."

Mingus tried to, but she couldn't find it in herself to smile. She just stood there.

"Would you like a seat?"

"Sit next to me," Tyson said, running over to the couch and plopping himself down on the middle cushion.

"No running, Ty, don't let me have to tell you that again."

"Sorry, Mama. You like Power Rangers?"

"I don't really know much about them."

Mingus walked over to the couch and sat down next to him.

"How about Giga Pets?"

"Nope, I don't know those either."

Tyson put his hand over his eyes and shook his head.

"I know you know how to play cowboys and Indians, everybody knows how to play that."

"I used to have a set of little plastic ones when I was a kid. I think they were brown."

"He's talking about the video game. Toys nowadays are either computerized or transform from a person into a spaceship or something."

Glenda stood only a few feet from Mingus, but Mingus kept her gaze on Tyson.

"Do you have any coloring books?"

"It's Power Rangers though, I can show you the right colors to use if you want."

"That would be nice, if you don't mind."

"I don't mind. Only we have to make sure Sarah doesn't eat my crayons. I'll be right back."

"That boy has too much energy and his attention span is that short," she said and snapped her fingers.

Mingus nodded, her expression still blank.

"Well, Sarah and I are going to finish up in the kitchen. Holler if you need anything."

She realized she shouldn't have come. Mingus sat on the green leather couch with her coat and gloves still on. It was too real. She had smelled Glenda's perfume in her nostrils; she could still smell it. It coated the butter and garlic smell coming from the kitchen. This was all too new. Too new to be as concrete as it was. Too new for a picture of her father with Glenda at some restaurant to be sitting on top of the console. She didn't know what she had expected, but this wasn't it.

"I couldn't find Power Rangers, but I have Hercules; it doesn't matter what colors you do this one."

"That sounds even better, Tyson." Mingus wiped her eyes with both gloves.

"Why do you call me Tyson? That name sounds funny."

"Because you told me I could. And it so happens that I like your name, it's a strong man's name."

"I'm still a kid, but whatever. Maybe when I get real big like thirteen I'll call myself Tyson."

As they colored, Ty sat Indian-style at the table and told Mingus about the spelling bee he had won and a fourth grader named Sonia who was trying to bribe him with Rice Krispies Treats to be her boyfriend.

"Is little Sonia a pretty girl?" Mingus asked.

"Yeah, as far as girls go. She's the second prettiest girl in our school and she's not little, she's tall. Maybe I'll let her be my girlfriend next year."

Mingus smiled and tapped the table.

"I'm finished."

"Okay," he said, perusing the page to make sure she was really done. "Now you gotta sign your name so everybody in the whole wide world knows who colored it. Like this."

Tyson wrote his name with a red crayon in big block letters along the top of the page. "Tyson Curtis Stewart. Now you gotta do yours."

Mingus picked a purple crayon from the yellow and green box and printed her name.

"There. Mingus Janay Browning. How's that?"

"Hey, your name is the same as my sister's. She scribbled on some of my pages, but I wrote her name for her 'cause she's a baby and she can't write yet."

"Really?" Mingus said, smiling at Tyson, adding a purple border around her picture, "what part of our name is the same?"

Tyson put both hands over his eyes again and shook his head at Mingus.

"Sisters always have the same last name, except for sometimes brothers don't. That's why when Dad adopts me I'm gonna have the same name too."

She couldn't understand what he was saying. Something was wrong with what she'd heard. Daddy? Sisters? Same name? Her heart palpitated in her chest.

"You mind showing me what you're talking about, Tyson?"

"Okay, if you really, really, really, really wanna see."

Mingus nodded.

"I'm gonna have to find my Power Rangers book then," Tyson said, getting up off his corduroy-covered knees. "And when we eat dinner you can wash your hands in my bathroom, okay? I have red soap and blue soap."

She nodded again. Her hands were sweating inside her gloves. He's just a boy, Mingus said, quieting herself. Boys make things up. Boys have overactive imaginations. He's just a boy. Just a boy.

"Now all we need is for Carl to get his tail back here. He probably stopped to return the videos or something." Glenda sat down in a wing chair near the living room window and stood the baby up on top of her legs. "You're trying to walk, huh? Yeah, Mama's precious. Oops, steady now."

Mingus stared at the back of the baby's slicked head. Her little feet making unsure steps. Her legs wobbling. She wanted to see the baby's face.

"Okay, here's my Power Rangers," Tyson said, running back into the room.

"What did I tell you about running in the house? I see I'm gonna have to get my switch, huh?"

"Sorry, Mama," Tyson said dully and sat down quietly on the couch next to Mingus. "See," he said in a low voice, "Sarah Marie Browning. I wrote it all by myself."

Glenda sat the baby down on her butt and walked over to the couch.

"Tyson! What are you doing?" She snatched the coloring book from Tyson's lap.

"I was just showing her that Sarah and her got the same name. That's all, Mama. Huh, Mingus?"

Tyson's face turned red. He stared up at Mingus, big question marks in his eyes.

"That's all, Tyson." Mingus gulped hard to keep her voice from shaking, "You didn't do anything wrong, okay?"

"See, Mama, I wasn't doing nothing."

Nervously, Glenda reached for Mingus, the coloring book in her right hand.

"Really, Carl was going to—"

"Don't say anything to me."

Mingus got up from the couch and started toward the door.

Glenda spoke to Mingus's back.

"He was going to tell you."

"He was going to tell me?" Mingus held onto the silver knob and turned her body toward Glenda. "When? Look at her, she's almost walking. When she's five he was going to tell me?"

"He didn't know how. He thought maybe if you started coming around it would be easier. You would see that—"

Glenda was pitiful to her. Her father was pitiful.

"You guys are liars." Mingus shook her head. "Both of you are liars. You don't know how to be honest. Either of you." Her voice was going hoarse. Mingus turned and fumbled with the lock with both hands.

"Where you going?" Tyson said, his voice sounding completely confused.

"I have to go home now, Tyson," she said, trying to grip her gloved fingers around the center dial of the lock. "I have to go home."

"But I thought you were gonna eat din—"

"Shush up."

"But Mama."

"Shush, Tyson. Just shush up."

Mingus felt the force of the door pushing open from the other side.

"Carl, I'm so glad you're home." Glenda rushed toward him and hugged him.

Mingus stared at the back of Glenda's head. She shook her head slow. She didn't want to cause a scene in front of the children. She just wanted to leave. And never see either of them again.

"She knows," Glenda said, holding both of Carl's hands. The bag of French bread dangled from his wrist. "Talk to her, Carl, she knows everything."

"Glenda, how did this—baby, let me explain. I was going to tell—" Tyson started to cry, followed quickly by Sarah.

"Sshhh, Tyson, it's okay," Mingus said, trying to add calm to her voice. Her father came toward her. "Don't touch me, I swear, don't touch me," she said, spreading her palms out in front of her.

He spoke softly. "Baby, please."

"You had every opportunity to tell me the other day. But you didn't. You just wanted to continue lying."

"Ming, I can explain."

"Don't you call me that. We were supposed to have a pact."

"Life doesn't always work under the same rules, Mingus."

Her head shook from side to side involuntarily.

"You were all I had. M'Dea has Eva. Now you have Sarah. I'm just—I'm leaving."

"Mingus, please. At least let me tell your mother myself. Please let me do that much."

"You should have thought about that a long time ago. Let me go."

His eyes were wet, along with everyone's in the house. He nodded his head and moved away from the door. Mingus walked out of the house hearing Eva's voice, mixed with Tyson's "What did I do?" and Glenda's "I'm sorry, I'm sorry." She had entered the enemy's camp and, like many traitors, she had lost the illusion that victory existed.

Chapter 38

Glenda asked me if I'd do it all again if I had to. I told her yes. She smiled and kissed me good on the lips. I don't think she got all of what I was meaning. Maybe she was just thinking about her part in my past. But who I was really thinking about was Ellie. In the same situation, I woulda married her again. Not in a heartbeat, but after thinking about it hard. It was the right thing to do. Right thing to do according to honor.

Bottom line, my family has been my life up till now. What else did I have? Things ain't been perfect, but can't nobody say I don't love them. Making myself something without a formal education, only thing that gets you this far is love or greed, and I ain't never been a greedy man. I have needs, and that's where Glenda entered in. But my needs have come last for all these years and I end up asking myself if I have the right to be happy.

It was easier when the kids were little. The sacrifice came more natural. Sometimes it came as easy as joy. Bouncing my girls on my lap. Teaching them how to hold a tune and read music. Working long hours to keep meat on the table. Those kind of things don't cost a person nothing. It's the quiet times after they grow up that cost. The absence of responsibility that makes you wonder why you're still sitting around. Fishing and hunting don't fix the lacking. Each thing you pick up to make the hole go away just makes it bigger. That's how I was living before I met Glenda. Always a few moments from being emotionally bankrupt.

Sarah and little Ty fill me. Remind me of my girls with all their energy and curiosity. Can't nobody wish children like that back. Only thing I can wish is to do better this time than I did last time.

Chapter 39

December 12

Every kingdom divided against itself is brought to desolation; and every city or house divided against itself shall not stand.

Matthew 12:25

She wasn't supposed to be on her period. Not on her birthday. Mingus turned over on her side and clicked the round knob on the lamp twice. She grabbed her journal from the nightstand and turned to the calendar section in the back of the book: 24th, 25th, 26th, 27th. Her period was way off. Being on the pill, early was damn near impossible. Period, every twenty-one days. No question marks.

She laid the journal on the pillow next to her and folded herself into a fetal position. Her head touching her knees, her arms wrapped around her stomach, the back of her ankles touching her buttocks.

Thirty isn't supposed to be like this. I was supposed to be together at thirty, she said to herself. A rumbling in the center of her abdomen split her body into two opposing halves. She was holding herself together with tears. Teardrops that seemed to relieve just enough pressure to allow her to breathe.

Instead of celebrating, all she could think about was her family and crayons. Crayons that etched another child's existence into hers. Bright red bold crayons that told her her father was a liar. The worst kind of liar, the kind who keeps secrets behind silence.

Mingus, no matter how she tried, couldn't stop the tears from falling. She couldn't stop the shaking of her uncombed head, the dull ache in the back of her throat that made it impossible to swallow. She couldn't stop wet sobs from seeping from her mouth or the sharp pulsing of her eyes under puffed eyelids.

She just kept seeing her name. Sarah Marie Browning, Sarah Marie Browning. Scribbled pages with big block letters. SARAH MARIE BROWNING. How could she have a sister and not know it? How could her father let her walk into that woman's house blind?

No, thirty wasn't supposed to be anything like this. She should have been sitting in front of the vanity, putting the finishing touches on her lipstick. This was supposed to be the big night; Mingus had felt it for weeks. She'd picked out a black catsuit and blazer. Black peekaboo lingerie with cutouts in the essential places. To Mingus, the mouth was sacred space. She had been saving that act for her husband. That was the one thing that she would give him that she had never given anybody else.

Mingus turned back toward the nightstand to check the alarm clock: 6:17. Eric would be there in less than two hours. All she needed was a few more minutes of rest, she told herself. Just a few more minutes and she would get up from bed after having lain there all day. A few more minutes and her body would stop aching and her head would still itself. She would get dressed and pack lingerie in the bottom of her purse. She would shower. She would return all the birthday wishes her machine had picked up. She would, in just a few more minutes.

When Eric arrived he had a crystal vase of yellow roses in his hand. He was sporting a black silk button-up shirt, black gabardine slacks, and matching double-breasted jacket. His head was shiny dark brown sugar bald from his new haircut. His goatee was shaved tight around lightly glossed lips. He unlocked the door and strolled into the bedroom.

Mingus was lying on her back, a sheet draped over her legs, uncovered from the waist up. Eric quietly sat the roses on the nightstand and leaned in over her breasts, cupping a nipple in his mouth. Mingus stirred and wiped his mouth away.

"Baby. You're still sleep." Eric nudged her waist.

Mingus focused her eyes then pulled the sheet up over her chest. With both hands she brushed stray pieces of hair from her face. "Hey."

"You were knocked out."

Eric caressed her cheek with the back of his hand. A trail of cologne crossed Mingus's nose. She thought of Glenda, how her perfume lingered in the living room even after she had gone back in the kitchen.

"I was just resting."

"You okay?"

Mingus rolled her neck to the left then the right. "I'm fine." She smiled. "I was really tired today."

"These roses were left at your door. I had them delivered this morning so I guess they've been sitting out there all day."

"They're beautiful. Yellow's my favorite." She wanted to hug him, but couldn't muster the energy to get up. She reached for his hand.

"You sure you're okay, baby? You don't seem like yourself."

"Maybe that's what thirty does to you. Changes you."

"Now I know you're not tripping. You're still a baby."

"Let you tell it." Mingus sensed the concern on his face. Maybe he really could tell something was wrong. "Eric, listen," she said, squeezing his hand. "Would you be disappointed if we postponed tonight? I really think—I just think I need to rest."

"Be real with me, Mingus, something happened."

She wanted to say no. That everything was just fine. She just needed to be alone for a while. Sort out a few details in her life. Mingus breathed deeply through her nose. Her heart was starting to fold in again.

"I have a sister." She zoomed in on his eyes.

"A sister besides Eva?"

"She's a baby. I wasn't even supposed to know about her."

"Your family is working you, huh?"

"M'Dea doesn't know. She shouldn't find out the way I did."

"Mingus, trust me, let your father handle this his own way."

"He's not in his right mind right now, and I'm too mad at him anyway. Look how he's handled things this far. I don't even know this baby. She doesn't know me. I've never held her."

"Baby, listen, today is your birthday. You need to let that stuff go. Pick it back up tomorrow if you have to, but let it go tonight."

"And my period just started. I wanted tonight to be romantic."

"Can you give me one second? I need to run down to the car right quick."

Mingus shrugged her shoulders. Soon as he turned his back, tears started to seep out of the corners of her eyes. She hated her life. She hated that everything had to look so ugly all at the same time. Eric was her one saving grace. She wiped her eyes on the corner of the pillowcase and reached for the small pastel yellow envelope attached to the roses.

Because your friendship is important to me;
because you are my closest confidante and companion;
because the sun rises in your smile—
because I love you, Happy Birthday Ming.
See you tonight.

Eric returned to the bedroom with three different-size boxes. All of them were wrapped in red-and-green paper with *happy birthday* written in gold cursive writing. He sat them on top of the jumbled blankets and walked back around to where he had been sitting at Mingus's waist.

"You're so beautiful," he said, touching the space where both her lips came together. Mingus felt currents move under his fingers. Currents that vibrated long after he had removed his touch.

"Thank you for the card." She sat up and wrapped the bedsheet snugly under her armpits. She took his hands between hers and held them tight. "You can't possibly know how much you being here has helped me the last few months."

"Don't flatter a brothah, this is *your* day."

"No, I'm serious." A fresh batch of tears collected in her eyes, she squeezed his hands tighter. "I couldn't have handled all this without you. You've been . . . just thank you, okay?"

Eric slid one of his hands from hers and grabbed the smallest gift from the stacked boxes.

"This is for you."

It was a palm-size box. Mingus ripped off the paper and opened the box, which held a four-inch-long, less than an inch wide plastic fish of some sort on a metal key ring.

"Interesting." Mingus smiled.

"It's a minireplica of the Dorado I caught when I went fishing. I bought it for you on my trip and honestly," he licked his bottom lip, "I had forgotten to give it to you when I got back so I decided to give it to you on your birthday."

"How considerate of you."

Mingus looked him in the eye and giggled.

"Hold the sarcasm, please. There is a rhyme to my reason. Open this one."

She opened it. A key. Two keys actually. She felt something strange tingling in her fingers.

"I've thought a lot about the talk we had on Thanksgiving. I just want you to know that I want you to have the keys to my home. I love you and you are welcome there anytime. I'm giving you these again so that you know that I know I didn't make a mistake the first time."

"Thank you." Her voice had diminished to a whisper.

"Okay, this one's next."

She opened the package and found a pair of jet-black sweatpants and matching sweatshirt. Mingus twisted a smirk on her face. "You trying to say something about the set I already have?"

"No, I like your other set. I just figure now you can have a black set and a gray set."

"My set *is* black."

Eric rolled his eyes. "This is the last one, you ready?"

"You're something else," Mingus said, slapping his leg. The box was the size of a nineteen-inch television. Mingus pulled the sheet higher around her chest and stood up on her knees in the bed. There was another box inside, this one the size of a thirteen-inch TV.

"You think you're smart, don't you," she said, starting to unwrap the second wrapped box. When she got to the bottom of the tissue paper, she pulled out a tiny palm-size box. She could hear her heartbeat. Mingus let out a breath and tried to catch it at the same time.

"Open it," Eric said.

Mingus snapped open the box. Earrings. Onyx surrounded by a circle of diamonds set in white gold.

"They're beautiful." She picked them up out of the box and noticed a folded piece of pastel yellow paper. "What's this?" Mingus said, sitting the earrings on the nightstand and looking at Eric. He shrugged his shoulders.

Mingus unfolded the note.

The real gift is in my pocket.
Love,
Eric

The tears started to flow and this time she couldn't stop them. "Don't play with me, Eric," she said, face contorted, her hair wildly circling her face.

Eric pulled Mingus back down onto her behind and held her hand as he kneeled in front of the bed.

"Mingus," he breathed, "I have never loved a woman the way I love you. You are my soul mate. I . . ." Tears hit his lips, Eric swallowed and held her hands tighter.

"Be my wife, Mingus. I will love you as I love myself. I will be faithful. I will believe you," he breathed, "I will be everything you need in a man. . . . Will you marry me?"

Mingus tried to but she couldn't speak.

"I know we've only known each other six months, but I know this is right. You can't put a time limit on what's right. I will be the best husband to you I know how to be. You have my word on that."

Mingus slid herself down to the carpet, her bare chest pressed against his shirt. She touched his face like it was her first time feeling skin under her fingers. She looked into his eyes as she traced his chin, his neck, back up to his lips. She kissed herself into him like she belonged there. Like she had always belonged there. Eric kissed her back, all ten of his fingers bracing her back.

"Yes," she said, nodding and speaking at the same.

Eric searched his inside breast pocket and pulled out a two-karat solitaire. He slipped it onto her ring finger.

"This is beautiful, I don't believe this." She was speaking to Eric but staring at the ring three inches from her face. "Oh my God, I don't even believe this."

Eric pulled himself up from the ground and pulled her up with him. Neither of them said anything. They just stood tied and knotted up in each other. Moment after moment, it was still real.

"I know you're tired; I'm gonna let you rest, okay."

"You don't have to go, Eric. I'm fine now."

"No, I want to," he said, pulling her head from his chest, holding her face. "I want you to have time to think about everything that just happened. I want you to be sure."

"Don't go." She squeezed his arm.

"I'm still down for tomorrow night, we can celebrate your birthday and our engagement."

"Okay, but early, like around four o'clock. Just so I know all of this is real. The earlier the better."

"It's real, Mingus." Eric kissed her forehead then lips. "It's real."

Mingus pressed her lips into his but kept her eyes open, believing that somehow, even after all of this, he could still disappear.

Chapter 40

We fell asleep together for the first time since Mingus and Eva were kids. When one of them was sick, I used to rub her body with eucalyptus oil and place a warm hot-water bottle on her chest to make her sweat the sickness out. With Mingus, after I swaddled her up tight, I'd slip one piece of butterscotch into her mouth to help her sleep. I'd drape my arm around her with the intention of getting back into my own bed once she dozed off. But somehow, when five o'clock came, I'd find myself cuddled up with my little girl.

Though you never want your child to be sick, those were some of the best times for me. We could be intimate without the slightest bit of awkwardness between us. I swear, I'd love her doubly hard during those days to make up for all the days I didn't when I should have. In the back of my mind, she was always her father's child more than she was mine. She'd act like him—pay attention to everything but comment little. Judge and juror syndrome I used to call it. It didn't surprise me that she became a lawyer. I think with the proper education, Carl would have been a damn good one himself.

Mingus was a sweet girl, always willing to help if she thought she was needed. She'd take out the trash for me and water the grass in the evenings if she didn't think I was going to get to it. But after a while, her silences intimidated me. Especially when she started with that journal. Sometimes when I was cleaning I'd look for it. She'd be at school and I'd find it under the bureau or behind the small bookcase in her room. She'd comment on an argument Carl and I had or how Eva shared half a bag of chips with her unexpectedly. One of my last times reading it, I found a picture Mingus titled "The Perfect Family" in big block letters. The scene was set in front of a square house with bright-green grass. There were four family members and each one was labeled. Mingus, Eva, Mom, and Dad. Everyone had a big, broad smile. The mother had long red hair like I did. She was tall and wore a floral dress. More than anything, what stuck out to me was the dark-brown faces and arms. I was hurt by seven-year-old innocence. I wondered if she really wanted a black mom instead of me.

I've thought about that picture a lot over the years. Knowing everything I do now, I think I understand Mingus better. What she really wanted was normalcy, a life without so many complications. As I look forward to my life again, that's all I'm really looking for as well. It's ironic to me that when I finally started to stand up for myself, Mingus came back to me. She could have gone to anyone else, but she came to me. That alone brought tears to my eyes. I held her to my chest and rocked her gently. She talked about Eric and Eva and being angry. I told her anger was good because at least she still felt something.

At some points over the last twenty years I had stopped feeling altogether. I was breathing but barely alive. I told her she was strong, whether she felt that way or not and that I'd never leave her again. I was sorry for not being a better mother. She was sorry for not knowing my favorite food and not including me in her life more. We sat on the couch all night holding each other. Nothing was erased; nothing was perfect, but it was good. Like I'd waited my entire life to see that clearly.

Chapter 41

December 13

She called him a dormant dog. Said like any other nigga all he needed was activation. I didn't believe her.

What if it had all been a dream? Mingus lay on her back, a burgundy-and-peach sheet of roses covering her body, a peach thermal blanket on top of that. The blinds were still drawn. The room was dark except for thin rays of light that slid sideways through overlapping strips of white plastic. Hands barely touching on her stomach, Mingus nudged her right hand over her left. It was still there. A solitary marquise diamond in a raised platinum setting.

She wanted to tell someone. She wanted to tell everybody but she couldn't. How can you tell your parents about your good news when their marriage is falling apart. Only person left was Eva. Mingus smiled. It would feel real once she spoke the words.

"Whatcha doing?" Mingus said, pacing in small circles, trying to conceal her excitement.

"I'm sleep, call me back."

"I need to talk to you right now."

"Look," Eva said and yawned into the phone, "I didn't get a chance to call yesterday 'cause I got in late last night. Happy belated, call me back."

"Can you spare two minutes?"

"If it has to do with that Negro of yours I don't want to hear it, especially not this morning."

"Why do you think it has to do with Eric?"

"Because, his pretentious ass probably bought you a new car or something."

Mingus giggled. "Better than a new car."

"I told you I don't want to hear about it."

"Come on, Eva, be happy for me."

"What?"

"First he gave me a key chain with his house keys on it, then he gave me some diamond earrings, then—"

"*Umph*. Sounds like a setup, if you ask me."

"What are you talking about?"

"Live-in pussy, that's what I'm talking about."

"You've never had the keys to a man's house before?"

"I ain't saying that. I'm saying ain't no nigga ever gave me house keys and a pair of diamond earrings in the same breath. I'm telling you it's a setup. Get you soft with the earrings so you can get him hard whenever he feels like it. Same thing kings used to do with courtesans, buy them gifts, make them feel special, then get unlimited, permanent pussy access."

"We already have sex, so what's the difference?"

"Watch." Eva smacked her lips. "It's about to go to a whole new level."

"Anyways, Eva, I wasn't finished."

"What, he straight out asked you to move in? This brothah's slick."

Mingus smiled and stared down at her finger. She said it in the sweetest, calmest voice she could muster.

"He asked me to marry him."

"You're lying?" Eva's voice raised two octaves.

"I'm dead serious."

"You didn't say yes, did you?"

"I wouldn't have the ring on my finger if I didn't say yes."

"Ohh well."

"*Oh well?* What is that supposed to mean?"

"It's your life, Mingus, you can mess it up if you want to. Don't expect me to throw you no damn ticker tape parade because of it."

"I don't get you. I really thought you would be happy for me. You know how much Eric means to me."

All Mingus could hear was Eva's breath. Seconds passed and Eva didn't say a word.

"You know what I think?" Mingus placed her hand on her hip. "I think you're jealous. You've been tripping on me and Eric ever since you started working for him."

"Pleeasse."

"I'm serious. You always get this way, whenever I do something before you do. It was like that with college, me starting my career, and probably a whole bunch of other situations I can't remember. Now marriage. You work with Eric, you know what a good man he is. Why can't you just be happy for me?"

"You've been smoking crack, sistah. Eric is a nigga, like all the rest of them."

"It's okay to be jealous, just admit it."

"You know what? I'm going to do you a favor and get off the phone before you get your little feelings hurt. 'Bye, Mingus."

Click. Mingus sat Indian-style on the bed and tried to figure out what had just happened. There was no good reason for Eva not to be happy for her. It was selfishness. Pure selfishness. Eva always seemed to hate Mingus worse when something good happened to her. She needed to talk to Eva in person. She needed things to be okay between them, at least for right now. Eva was the only person she had besides Eric. Mingus threw on her coat and the black sweatsuit Eric had bought her and made her way to Eva's neighborhood in less than twenty minutes.

"Eva, it's Mingus, open up," she yelled, looking directly into the peephole. "Look, if you can prance by unannounced, I expect you to return the favor. I'm not leaving until I talk to you."

No answer. Mingus sat down in the covered door well and pulled her black knit cap over her ears. After what felt like ten minutes Eva partially opened the door. A gold metal door chain draped across her forehead.

"Why's the chain on?"

"Because I don't want to talk to you right now, Mingus."

"Why not, Eva?"

"I don't have anything to talk to you about so you're wasting your valuable time, Miss Lawyer."

"I have something to say."

"Feel free to spill your guts on my door step—if you don't mind my neighbors listening. You know how nosey black folks can be. Sister-girlfriend next door will have your business on the green line by noon."

"Let me in, Eva. You said no more games between us, what's this?"

"Look, my place is a mess, I wasn't expecting company."

"I didn't come here to check out your kitchen, I came to talk to you." Mingus ran both hands briskly up and down her forearms. "It's cold out here."

Eva rolled her eyes. "Give me a second."

After five minutes Eva reopened the door. She'd changed the place around since the last time Mingus had been inside.

"You bought a new couch, the brown leather complements the design in the throw pillows."

"It's not new, it's used. I bought it at a secondhand store."

"It's new to you," Mingus said.

"If that's the case there's a lot of new shit around here. Did you expect me to keep your old hand-me-downs forever?"

Eva was doing it again. Trying to incite an argument so that

Mingus would get mad and leave. Mingus walked across the squeaky wooden floor and sat down on the couch. She pressed her palms into the cushions.

"It's in good shape."

"I take it you're staying?" Eva stood hand on hip, back against the wall, freestyling a half-buttoned man's dress shirt.

"It's toasty in here." Mingus took off her cap and balled it between her hands. "Cute shirt."

Eva rolled her eyes and switched from hand on hip to crossed arms.

"Why are you here?"

"I'm sorry for saying you were jealous, Eva. I know I came on strong and I'm sorry. I just want you to be happy for me. You're the only sister I have. I was kinda hoping that we could squash the history between us and you'd consider being my maid of honor. Really, Eva, the person you've been hating for all these years is the little girl you used to know. I'm grown up now. You've grown up. Things should be different between us."

"We're not sisters, Mingus. We're relatives. And you live in a fantasy world. This is not the damn magic kingdom, our past doesn't disappear the moment you get a ring on your finger." Eva laughed. "And you think because a man shows you some attention he ain't a dog. A nigga is a nigga is a nigga is a dog. You need to accept that."

Mingus's cheeks started to burn from the inside out.

"You don't know what you're talking about."

Eva pulled a piece of Juicy Fruit from her shirt pocket and unwrapped the metallic paper. She pressed both ends of the stick together then popped it in her mouth.

"Only difference between a dormant dog and a full-time dog is activation."

Mingus shook her head.

"Are you that unhappy, Eva?"

"Who's really unhappy, huh? I don't worry about anything, Mingus. I just handle my business and take the consequences as they come. There's always fallout. But your ass is too busy trying to create the perfect family and the perfect sister and the perfect husband to even see what your life really looks like."

She was absolutely sick of Eva. There was no point. Mingus placed her knit cap back on her head and stood up.

"Buckle up and drive safely," Eva said, walking ahead of Mingus to the door.

"Could you manage to get me a glass of water before I leave?"

Eva popped a bubble hard in her mouth.

"Can't you stop at the liquor store down the street?"

"You are something else," Mingus said.

"I'm out of drinking water."

"Tap is fine, I just need to wet my throat."

Eva rolled her eyes again.

"Wait here."

She disappeared through the swinging double doors. Mingus walked after her into the kitchen.

"Dammit." Eva's jawbone twitched. "I told you to stay out there."

"What's the big deal? I just want some water, shoot me, why don't you."

"Drink the water and go, Mingus."

She handed Mingus the ribbed plastic cup. Water sprinkled onto the arm of her coat. Mingus placed the cup on the counter. That's when she noticed them. Empty Black Velvet bottles. Peppering the counters. Sitting atop dirty dishes in the sink.

"What's this?" Mingus said, shaking droplets of water from her hand.

"You know what, just get the hell out of my house." Eva knocked the cup of water into the sink with the back of her hand. Water splashed the thin white curtains making gray splotches.

"You drank all these by yourself?" Mingus reached for a bottle on the counter but Eva grabbed it first.

"You think you're so fucking smart, don't you? I hate you, I swear to God I hate you."

Lines furrowed in Eva's forehead. A small mountain ridge gathered between her eyes.

Strangely, Mingus felt better about her sister. At least the alcohol was an explanation. She could help Eva fix that. Then maybe things could be better between them.

"You need help, Eva. I can find a rehab before the weekend is over. Don't even worry about your apartment and stuff, I can take care of everything while you're gone." Mingus reached for Eva's shoulder but Eva slapped her hand away.

"You make me sick." Eva balled up her fists at her side. "Get out of my house."

Mingus pulled off her cap and leaned her hand on the counter. "I'm not leaving, Eva, not until we talk about this and figure out what we're going to do. I think you should definitely consider rehab, I know Eric would hold your job if he knew what was going on."

"Fuck you and Eric." Spittle landed from Eva's mouth onto Mingus's lip. "You think you have the situation all figured out, don't you? You're so slow, Ming. Isn't that what he calls you? You're so busy trying to fix other folks' problems when you can't even handle your own. Matter of fact, you don't even see your own. Did you ever stop to think that there was a reason Eric was so gung-ho about introducing me to his brother? Or that maybe there's a *reason* he feels so comfortable around me?"

Mingus didn't say anything. She just wiped the white food particles from her lip.

Eva's mouth tightened as words jerked from it.

"No of course not. I forgot, you're Miss Fantasyland."

"Shut up, Eva, this is about you. I'm trying to help you."

"Maybe this is about *you,* ever think about that?" Eva tapped the empty bottle in her palm like a baton.

"Just shut up."

Eva smiled.

"Oh, you don't like it when the shoe is on the other foot. It's okay when you're all up in my business, but you can't handle when your shit stinks, can you?"

"You're just trying to upset me. You're mad because I'm getting married."

"Mingus, your life is hanging by a thread. You're so needy. I need a sister, I need a this, a that. What's it been, a few months with Eric? Why the hell would a man with everything going for himself just up and propose? He barely knows you."

Eva tapped the bottle slower. The thick black glass fell into her hand like a gavel.

"Fine, Eva. You want to drink your pitiful life away, I'm not going to try to stop you. You should have learned in high school, but you'd rather blame someone else for your messups."

Mingus grabbed her cap from the counter and headed for the door. Eva followed steps behind her.

"Oh wait." Eva spoke in feigned innocence. Mingus could feel Eva's breath on the side of her face. "I think I figured it out, Mingus. Maybe he's been having an affair with your sister. Maybe that's why he proposed. So by the time the shit hit the fan he'd have you hooked. But you probably don't want to hear that, huh? Let's just ignore it and concentrate on poor alcoholic Eva. Poor, poor confused Eva."

She inched closer. Her breath was hot and smelled of liquor and chewing gum. Mingus stood, face almost touching the door, hand barely extended from her waist on the doorknob. There were no gloves this time. All she had to do was turn the knob. Turn the knob and leave.

"Are you telling the truth?" Mingus said into the door.

"Why would I lie, Mingus?" Her voice was seductive.

"Because you want to hurt me, because I know about your alcohol problem. Because I know why you lost your job."

" 'Because I know about your alcohol problem.' " Eva pushed her chest into Mingus's back. "I don't care what you know anymore. I'm tired of trying to be perfect for you."

"I never asked you to be perfect, I'm not perfect."

Mingus kept her eyes trained on the peephole. She wanted to turn around. She wanted to look into Eva's eyes and see that she was lying.

"What did Daddy used to call you? His perfect little princess. Guess you're gonna have to tell Daddy how mean old Eva destroyed your engagement."

"I don't believe you." Mingus could hear the slow rhythmic tapping of the bottle.

"He enjoyed it, Mingus." She pressed hard into Mingus, her lip touching her ear. "Said he's never had a woman make him come like that before."

Mingus pulled the door open, knocking them both into the wall and never looked back.

"Ask him, why don't you ask him!" Eva yelled from the door well. The sidewalk was a gray blur. Mingus grabbed her keys from her coat pocket. The muscles in her thighs tightened with each step. *He enjoyed it,* looped through her head. *He enjoyed it.* She drove, not knowing where to go. She didn't want to go home. She couldn't go home, not yet. Even though Eva was lying. She had to be lying. Eric loved her, he would never do that. He just wouldn't. Mingus drove. Unable to find tears, unable to find a voice. Just a numbing tension in her fingers. A throbbing in the sides of her head. He wouldn't do it. He wouldn't.

She tried to keep herself from thinking back. Back to Eric squeezing Eva's waist. Back to the red dress. Back to the attitude Eva would have when Mingus called Eric at work. Mingus needed someone to save her. Someone who could fill her up before the pain came. The real pain this time. She landed in M'Dea's driveway.

"Mingus," M'Dea said, opening the door with a surprised smile.

All she could do was stand there.

"Are you okay?"

She shook her head no. M'Dea pulled her into the house and closed the door behind them.

"You need to sit down. Is it your father? What's wrong, baby, don't scare me like this." M'Dea held Mingus's hand and led her to the couch. As soon as M'Dea sat down, she popped back up. "Let me get you some water."

Water. Water caused the breaking of her world. One single glass of water.

"Don't leave," Mingus said, pulling M'Dea by the hand back down to the couch.

"You're safe, baby. It's okay, whatever it is."

Mingus held her mother's hand tight. She wasn't safe. She could still see Eric's arm around Eva's waist. She could still feel Eva's lip warm on her earlobe. *He enjoyed it, Mingus.*

Mingus cried hard. Heaving flooded her chest in jerking waves. The pain was too great to hold back, her world was too fragile.

"Baby? What? Please don't do this."

M'Dea grabbed her face and shook her. The shaking caused slobber to loose from Mingus's lips.

"Are you hurt?" M'Dea said frantically.

Mingus nodded yes. She looked M'Dea in the eye through flowing tears.

"Eva, Mama."

"Eva?" M'Dea said, still holding Mingus's face. "Is Eva okay?"

"She—"

Mingus couldn't say it. The thought of saying it hurt too much.
"What Mingus?"

Mingus shook her head, rattling teardrops from her eyes.

"Eva. Eric, Mama."

"Eva and Eric? Your man friend?" M'Dea stared into Mingus's
eyes; Mingus nodded. "Oh, no. Baby." M'Dea pulled Mingus into
her chest. She held her tightly in her arms. Even with Mingus's
coat on, M'Dea managed to get her arms completely around her.
She knew. Mingus didn't even have to say it. M'Dea knew, just by
looking into her eyes.

"He proposed last night," Mingus said into M'Dea's chest.
"I told him yes. I was so happy. Now I can't and I want to so
badly. I love him so much. He's good to me." M'Dea stroked
Mingus's hair. "I don't know if I should believe her, but Eva
doesn't lie."

"Shh," M'Dea said into Mingus's hair.

"I don't know what to do," Mingus said.

M'Dea held her tighter.

"You're going to calm down and you're going to find out the
truth."

"I don't want to know the truth; I want to marry Eric."

"You're strong, baby. When you're ready, you're going to find
out what happened and then you'll make the right decision, whatever it is."

The touches were soothing. Reminded Mingus of how Eric
stroked her hair as they lay in bed talking at night.

"I can't lose him, M'Dea," she said calmly, "not right now. I
couldn't take that right now."

"Listen, baby, I served your father divorce papers. You're the
one that told me I should do it. To protect my interest. The day
you told me that, I couldn't even fathom doing it. But I did it. Not
overnight. I progressed to it."

"I'm not that strong."

"You'll get that strong then. You're going to do the right thing, Mingus; I know that in my heart."

Mingus didn't know. But she had to trust somebody, and at that point, if she couldn't trust herself, M'Dea was the next closest thing.

Chapter 42

I hadn't spoke to Ellie in a week of Sundays. Hadn't even gone by to pick up my clothes. Managed by poppin' a load of the necessaries into the washer every few days to keep me goin'. Glenda picked me up some odds and ends every so often when she was out.

I got this feeling in my gut that the whole situation was gonna work itself out. Soon as everybody's emotions and sensibilities had time to settle back into place. Glenda was already acting pretty normal again. More normal even. She fired the gardener who kept up her lawn and asked me to do it. Even though it was winter, she was already making plans, looking for us to be like a real family. And far as I could see, we looked pretty official. I was fixin' stuff around the house, taking care of the kids when she had errands to run. Usually everything felt pretty good. Like I was finally in the right place.

But sometimes, I would get that missing feeling. Like a chain on a bike with too much slack. I would be sitting around listening to the day Glenda had at work or how many sales she made. Maybe watching Tyson teach Sarah how to use his old building blocks. Outta nowhere, I would get the desire to get up and run. Just pack up the stuff I had left and when no one was looking, run like hell fire was on my heels. And I don't know where I woulda went. Every time I thought about it, the outcome was different. Sometimes it would be back to my mama's house. Sometimes it would be to some small hick town where I could pick up some hand tools and make me a living. And then sometimes, a whole bunch of times, it was right back to Ellie. Her sitting up on the couch knitting blankets for grandchildren that ain't been born yet. Me reclined in my La-Z-Boy filling out a crossword puzzle or picking up a game on the tube.

It was on one of them days, one of them days that I was thinking 'bout Ellie that my stuff came. Not just my clothes, but it seemed like everything I owned was on that moving truck. My hunting rifles, my recliner, my tools from the tool shed. My razors, my high blood pressure medicine, my business files. All my records—Sarah, Carmen, Charles, John, Dizzy, Al, and everybody else. Ellie had hired on two college boys to pack up my stuff and bring it right to Glenda's front door step. Ellie and me had been living in that house for over twenty years, musta took her weeks to get all that stuff together.

Glenda answered the door with hands-on-hip attitude, told the red-headed, crew cut-wearing boy that there musta been some mistake. But he just read down the work order: Delivery for Carl Browning, 1065 Redvine Avenue. Wasn't too much you could mistake about that. Wasn't no mistakin' that that was my stuff in the back of that truck. No mistakin' where it had come from or who had sent it. Glenda stared back at me as I sat back on the couch with the Sunday newspaper, stared that your-black-ass-better-do-something-right-now look. I slipped my loafers back on my feet and grabbed both sets of keys off the hook in the kitchen. Moved Glenda's car to the street, then mine, but all the time I was thinking about Ellie. Thinking about how somewhere, in one of them boxes or black plastic garbage bags she'd stuffed my belongings into, somewhere, I'd also find a nine-by-twelve manila envelope that still held divorce papers.

Chapter 43

December 14

I didn't find the note until a week later. Eric had Scotch-taped it to my freezer door. Said he had gotten to my place at four and waited for me until seven o'clock. Said he figured I had gotten caught up with my family because of my birthday and the engagement. Said even though he understood, I owed him big time, I twisted the lined paper into a twig and burned it under the pan of eggs as I scrambled.

She woke up to pounding. The chain on the door was stretched to its limit and Eric was trying to knock the chain from its track with a screwdriver. Mingus had fallen asleep on the couch, curled up in her coat and sweatsuit. The soles of her tennis shoes left traces of dried mud on the arm of the couch. She should have never given him her keys, she thought, watching through swollen slits as his hand maneuvered the screwdriver.

Mingus hoped he would lie, but more than that, she hoped that she'd believe him completely as he did it. That he'd laugh hard in her face then wrap her curls around his index finger and tell her that never in a thousand years could he hurt her that way. Then he'd say everything again. That she was the only woman he needed in his life, that he loved only her. That he'd scream it to the top of his lung forever if he had to.

"Mingus, I know you're in there, otherwise the door wouldn't be bolted and your car wouldn't be parked outside. . . . Baby please, just say something. Let me know you're okay."

Lyingsonofabitch.

"Are you getting cold feet? Whatever it is, we can talk about it. Please, just be okay. Say something."

"Leave me alone, Eric."

"Praise God," he said, removing the screwdriver from the door.

"You have no right to praise God. Get away from my door."

"Mingus? What's wrong with you? Baby, why are you trippin'?"

"Get away from my door!"

"I'm not leaving." Eric stuck the screwdriver back in the door and pulled. "I just proposed to you, do you remember that? It's me, Eric Simms, your fiancé."

"You're a liar."

He paused.

"You're so pathetic, the both of you are," she said.

"Mingus, let me in, let's not do this in front of your neighbors. It's Sunday morning, people are sleeping."

Tears dripped from the corner of her left eye across her nose and down her right cheek. The outer lining of the comforter stuck to her face. She couldn't go on this way.

"Move the screwdriver, Eric." Mingus closed the door and unbolted the lock. Her eyes were almost completely shut. Eric reached out to cup her cheeks.

"Mingus, your face."

"Why did you sleep with my sister, Eric?"

"Whoa, Mingus—hey, I didn't sleep with Eva." He stuck his flattened palms out shoulder level and looked her in the eyes.

Mingus shook her head. Throbbing tensed her forehead. "Don't lie to me."

"I didn't, Mingus. I promise I didn't."

"You didn't sleep with Eva?" She looked into his bulged eyes.

"No, Mingus, I didn't."

"Why did she tell me that?"

"Mingus, I—I don't know. You said yourself you thought she had a crush on me."

Something was wrong. Mingus walked back over to the couch and held her head between her hands. "You didn't have an affair with Eva, Eric?"

"I promise you, Mingus, I didn't, you have to believe me."

"What happened, then?"

Tiny beads of sweat surfaced on his forehead. Eric wiped his face with both hands. "It's all a big misunderstanding."

"Then something did happen?"

"This situation, this whole situation. I love you, Ming, I need—"

"Fuck you, Eric, you can't even tell me the truth. You don't love me and go screwing around with my sister. You can't even admit it, and that's the absolute least you could do. At least then I could stop hating you. At least then there might be even the tiniest possibility of us maintaining some kind of relationship."

"It wasn't my fault, Mingus, I swear it."

Mingus pretended to be calm, but inside she was folding in. "What happened?"

"I never wanted your sister. I gave her a job because, you know why I gave her a job, I wanted to help you. You were my reason for everything—"

"What happened, Eric?"

"Can I sit down?"

Mingus pointed to the love seat. Eric sat down on the edge of the cushion and leaned forward toward her. "Remember after you met my family, you were worried about her having a crush on me?" His hands paused midair with his question. "Well, I thought you were right, so I figured I'd talk to her and nip the situation in the bud. It was the night before we were filming the big Christmas show. That was my first big show with the TV station and I wanted it to be good. I had to stay late, I didn't really have a choice, there were so many loose ends to tie up before filming the next morning.

"Eva volunteered to stay late with me. I probably would have asked her to anyway, because she was my assistant, not for any other reason. It was important for me to handle the crush situation, but I wanted to finish detailing the show first. Just in case we got in some big argument, at least the work would be done.

"It was, I don't know, maybe around seven-thirty when we finished. Just about all of the day crew had cleared out. I asked Eva to come into my office."

As he spoke, Mingus closed her eyes and visualized what happened.

" 'Eva, can I speak to you in my office?'

" 'You're always trying to give me more work, I'm already staying late.'

" 'No, I just need to speak to you before you leave out of here tonight.'

" 'Sounds serious.'

" 'Nothing to stress out over.'

" 'Right now is as good a time as any—'

"I'm telling you Mingus," he said, tapping his right foot in short, quick motions, "my intentions were only professional. Eva kept trying to bait me with little innuendoes."

"Just tell me what happened."

"I told her that you were having a problem with her working with me because you thought that she was trying to get at me.

" 'Look, Eva,' I said, 'I'm going to shoot straight with you. Mingus doesn't feel comfortable with you working for me. She feels like you have a crush of some sort on me and that I need to talk to you about it.'

" 'Okay that's what this is about, you're trying to appease Mingus.'

" 'Yes and no. I'm just trying to get to the heart of the situation so that I can decide what to do next.'

" 'Oh, so you're thinking about firing me, then?'

" 'I'm not saying that either. Worse comes to worse, there's an opening on the morning show, I would give you a stellar recommendation.'

" 'I don't believe this. Your little girlfriend gets a strange feeling and you want to fire me because of it. She can't run the whole world, and get people fired because of her *feelings*. Did you tell her that?'

" 'Look, Eva, let's just get down to it; what are your intentions here?'

" 'I don't believe this, my intentions are to work and get paid, Eric. Remember I didn't approach you about this damn job, you guys approached me.'

" 'Okay, then it's settled.'

" 'So you're saying that if I did have some attraction to you, you would fire me?'

" 'We have the situation settled, let's just leave it at that.'

" 'Just hypothetically. I mean you are hella fine, can't nobody take that way from you. Strong legs. Lord knows you shouldn't be allowed to wear no jeans around here. Shit, I'd take a piece.'

" 'Okay, Eva, good night, it's time for you to go—'

"Then she stood up, Mingus. She had on one of those minidresses. She reached under and unsnapped both sides of her panties so that they fell to the ground. I was shocked, all I could do was sit there on the edge of my desk.

" 'What if I just take a piece, hum, Eric? You wouldn't stop a sistah from free enterprise, would you? You wouldn't. I can tell from the eyes. What, you want these?' She reached down and picked up the panties and held them to her nose. 'You wanna smell it?'

" 'Okay, Eva, I've had enough, you gotta go.'

" 'Unh, uh . . .'

"Then she stepped closer to me, Mingus. I couldn't believe it. She's your sister, I swear, I couldn't even grasp what was going on. She asked me why I wasn't moving, asked me if I was afraid of little old her. She came closer to me, Mingus, almost between my legs and I stopped her. I grabbed her by her shoulders and asked her why she was doing it, if she was trying to ruin our relationship. I told her point blank that she was fired and to get out of my office. Then she changed. She started crying, Mingus. Said she didn't know why she did it, that she was just so mad at you for accusing her of such a thing that she wanted to get even with you. She was crying, asking me please not to fire her. I felt bad. I told her she could keep her job but that she couldn't ever trip out like that again, upset or not. She got happy again. She instantaneously gave me a big hug and thanked me."

Mingus could see Eric sitting on the edge of the desk, consoling Eva. The two of them wrapped up in each other. Eva's bare legs between Eric's thighs. Eric scrunching her panties to his nose.

"Then she changed again, Mingus. I swear. She pressed her body into my chest and reached down for my zipper. I pushed her shoulders. She kept coming. I asked her what she was doing. She just kept mumbling nothing, nothing, until finally my penis was in her hand. Mingus, I swear I tried to grab it away. I—

" 'Eric, what a wonderful surprise, do you feel how hard it is?'

" 'Get off me, Eva.'

" 'Okay, just give me one more second, and I promise, I'll leave you alone—'

"Then she bent at the waist and then out of nowhere she started sucking it."

"I've heard enough, Eric." Mingus shook her head. "I don't want to hear it."

"Mingus, at least let me finish. I want you to see what really happened. It wasn't my fault. I tried to push her off of me. She had my dick in her mouth, she locked her arms around my waist and wouldn't let go. I was stuck, don't you understand?"

"Bullshit, Eric, bullshit. I can't believe you're putting me through this." She stood up and held her arms over her chest. "If this is how it happened, if she forced herself on you and you fought her off, why didn't you just fire her and come to me immediately? You could have come to me; why didn't you say something?"

"How could I say something about that? It took you forever just to tell me about you kissing that white boy."

"I'm not even going to acknowledge that. At least if you had told the truth, I coulda— You lied and covered things up, just like she did."

"I needed to think, Mingus. Figure out what to do next. You can't even imagine what I was going through."

"You are something else. Have you thought about everything I'm going through right now? Do you see how messed up my life is now? At least if you would have told me before, I wouldn't have been so dumbfounded when I went over Eva's yesterday to show her my engagement ring. What a joke. I wouldn't have even been over Eva's if—"

"I couldn't tell you, Mingus, why can't you hear me? She was holding it over me."

"Right, big old Eva holding it over you."

"I came." His voice lost his power and registered a little more than a whisper.

"What?"

"I came, Mingus."

"Get the hell out of my house, Eric."

"Please, just keep listening to me."

"Get out!" She grabbed the glass vase that had been emptied of roses off the coffee table and held it over her head with both hands. "Get out and I swear, don't you ever come back."

"Mingus, it was quick, it happened before I even knew it. Thirty seconds. Come on, it's not like something like that happens to me every day. I couldn't believe any of it. Can't you see that I love you and I would have never chosen for any of this to happen?"

"I can't see anything right now. Just go, Eric. I'm tired."

He got up and walked over to her. "I messed up, but not like you thought. I didn't have sex with your sister, I didn't have an affair with her, I didn't want her."

"No, you just came in her mouth."

"Mingus, why won't you listen to me. Don't you hear what I'm saying? It's not a reason to end our relationship."

"You're not the person who gets to decide that."

"If you can't do anything else, just look me in the eyes. My eyes won't lie to you, they can't."

He inched closer to her and held her face in his hands.

"Look at me."

His hands were soft against her skin.

"What do you see, Mingus?"

"Nothing, Eric. You lied to me."

"Look close."

"I don't feel you anymore, Eric."

"Just like that?"

"Go, Eric."

"Tell me it's over, Mingus. Look me in my eyes and tell me it's over and I'll leave you alone."

She looked into his eyes. All she could see was love. She saw her future there. He was supposed to be the one. She loved him. She always would, just as she had promised.

"It's over."

It took a long time before he finally dropped his hands from her face and walked out. He just kept looking back at her. Mingus locked the door behind him.

Chapter 44

I still remembered the address: 283 Brand Street, space 29, Wilmington, North Carolina. I remembered it like I still lived there and my room was still in place. Grade cards taped to the back of my closed door. Twin bed shoved into the right corner of the fake wood grain wall. Two-foot-high, five-foot-long window above my bureau. The unframed mirror with the silver paint chipping off the back, so that when I looked at myself, my image would be shallow where the paint had peeled. The black iron imprint at the foot of my bed covered by the oval throw rug, its thick round cords alternating beige then brown, beige then brown.

I'd stay in my room and my mama used to stay in the kitchen. Preparing a meal for me and my father, maybe a homemade meat pie or chicken and stuffed dumplings. I know now that those meals were as much for her as they were for us. Maybe more for her. There's something about rolling cool dough under your fingers. Shaping, cutting. Flour on your face and apron. There's something about it that tunes you into yourself. Nothing else really exists in those moments. No problems, no heartbreak. Just the power of your fingers, just your taste buds and your judgment. No one else's. I know now that there is power in the kitchen, that's why I've been drawn to it all these years. I can create myself over and over again in there. Bake myself into casseroles, fresh rosemary bread, a lemon cream pound cake. I can become everything I can't be anywhere else. So many forms of beautiful. Just like my mother used to do, standing for hours at the stove.

I missed her. Out of everything that used to be my life, everything I'd given up, I missed my mother so badly. So bad. I just wanted to curl myself into her and cry into her full bosom, let her hold my face and kiss my forehead right smack in the center and pull me into her. I wanted to feel her arms soft around my back, smell the vanilla and cinnamon baked into her skin. I wanted to look her in the eyes and see that she wasn't angry at me, that she had forgiven me for leaving. Forgiven me for never saying good-bye. I needed to see myself in someone. Someone who had my eyes and my nose, my hair. My skin. My smile. I needed to appear somewhere. I couldn't take existing anymore in the secret life of someone who couldn't love me back.

Chapter 45

December 20

Sometimes it's the little things, like feeling my heartbeat or hearing myself breathe, that make me know I'm not supposed to die like this.

Mingus could hear Eva's voice. Barreling through silence like it was hers. Vibrating through the closed door like she was entitled to break sanctity. Mingus sat on the couch in her coat, sweatsuit and tennis shoes blending in with early evening shadows. She hadn't bathed. Her socks made elastic imprints around her ankles. She sat Indian-style, ankles crossed above her knees, hands folded in her lap.

She watched the ceiling. Watched how Merlot gelled red at the bottom of an empty wineglass. Watched how yellow plant leaves laid flat in springy green foliage. If she sat really still, nothing moved. Nothing changed. And maybe if she sat like that forever, nothing would ever change again.

"Look, girl, open the door. I'm sorry."

If nothing ever changed, Mingus thought, then nothing would ever happen. Hurt couldn't seep any deeper and trust could be used as cow manure.

"Look, Mingus, it's not Eric's fault. I shouldn't have even said anything about it. I was being spiteful. I was mad 'cause you thought you could dictate my life just because Eric was your man. You remember how you asked for time off for me for M'Dea's anniversary . . . I was angry. I wanted to get you back. Mingus! Are you there! We didn't have an affair. It was just that one thing."

Thing. It's funny how *things* sound so harmless. If it would have been anyone else but Eva, maybe. Not her sister.

"I'm quitting my job, Mingus. Can't you just open the door? I'm not going to be around there anymore. You guys can just pick up where you left off."

Mingus could silence Eva's knocking, just like everything else. Just like the phone calls, just like the liars talking into the tight space between the door and frame. *Click.* Everything off. Only thing that mattered was silence. And teardrops, but only sometimes.

"I came to bring by your Christmas gift. I made it myself. And I wrapped it this time. Actually I bought one of those decorated bag things and put some green-and-white tissue paper in it. You'll know why I made it if you open it. If nobody steals it from your door. But I guess things like that don't happen in your neighborhood.

"You gonna make me stand here? It's a few days before Christmas, I don't have to tell you it's cold outside . . . I'm sorry. I wouldn't have said anything if you wouldn't have stopped by with a damn ring and bogarted into my kitchen. It relaxes me, the alcohol. I'm not gonna lie about it. This world is hard sometimes. Especially when you're just trying to pay your bills and survive. Mingus . . . I don't know what else to say."

Sometimes you have to stop talking. You just breathe. Breathe and hope the madness doesn't take you over.

"I'm not looking for you to forgive me and just start over like nothing happened . . . I'm not going to rehab, but I did start going to AA, every day for the last four days. I don't know about this opening-up, honesty thing. Seems like it just makes more problems. Anyways. I'm not gonna stand out here all night. I just wanted to bring this by and say I was sorry. . . . Yeah, that's all. I love you."

Just breathe, Mingus thought. Breathe and honor the teardrops.

Chapter 46

Dear Mama,

This is Elaine, I know you haven't heard from me in a long time. I'm sorry for that. I had all these reasons why I couldn't call and why I couldn't come back and why you never wanted to see me again. I can't remember any of them anymore. I can't remember what could have been so important to keep me away from you for so long. I miss you, Mama. With all my heart.

I'm okay. I've had some bad things happen to me, but I'm okay. I've just been thinking about you. How you loved me so much, how you believed in me. I want you to know that I still have the dress you made me for graduation. Beautiful, beautiful pearl white it was. The gold buttons on it still shine. As you must imagine, I can't fit it anymore. I've grown a bit. I stopped wearing those short pageboy haircuts. My hair is long now. Almost to the center of my back, like yours was the last time I saw you.

You have two granddaughters, Mingus and Eva. Eva's the oldest, the one I was pregnant with when I left home. I named her after you. They're both beautiful. You'll be proud to know that Mingus is a lawyer and Eva works for a television network as a production assistant. They're both very bright.

Carl and I aren't together anymore. I guess Dad would say he was right all along. Kind of ironic now that I think about it. The way everything turned out. I loved him, Mama. I swear I did. I thought I was doing the right thing. We were gonna raise this wonderful family and I was going to prove Dad wrong. I shouldn't have—there's so many things I should have done differently. It's funny how they're all hitting me now so clearly.

I have a nice house, Mama. There's a little lake with fish in it and a whole bunch of trees and sweet smells. I know you would love it here. I have a big, big kitchen. Tiled counter space, my oven bakes on both sides. Sometimes I make homemade dumplings like you used to do. Mine taste almost as good.

I'm sorry, Mama, I'm really, really sorry. I wasted all this time not talking to you, not sending you pictures, not hearing your voice. I tried calling our old number, but of course it was disconnected. I was nervous when I picked up the phone anyway. And then of course I thought about the possibility that maybe you moved from the old place or Dad sold the trailer. I really hope that's not the case, Mama. I hope you get this. I hope you're well and strong. I know that you are. You are Mama, you have to be. If it won't upset him too much, tell Dad I said hello. Please write me back or call. Please, as soon as you get this.

Your daughter,
Elaine O'Brien Browning

Chapter 47

She got in by using the key under the back doormat. M'Dea wasn't there. Mingus checked every room before settling on the couch. That's when she remembered the car M'Dea had bought. She breathed. She had only pulled herself together for the purpose of telling M'Dea about Sarah. Then she would go back home and fall apart again.

She removed her arms from her coat and leaned her face over the glass in the coffee table. Her eyes were puffed. Even her nose and lips. She stared at her reflection, wondering how anybody could love a face that looked like that. After a few moments her peripheral vision picked up pieces of the collage scattered about her. All the pictures spread out on the table were of her and Eva. It seemed strange to her, like M'Dea had been conducting some sort of experiment. Intermixed with the photographs were snippets of photocopied facial features. Mingus noticed her mouth and eyes, Eva's nose, cutouts of their father. M'Dea had pasted a patchwork face onto a piece of orange construction paper. A Face that looked like no one she knew but at the same time felt familiar. The tape case was labeled CARL'S OTHER FAMILY. It sat on the edge of the table empty atop a manila envelope. It's spine blaring block letters in Mingus's direction. She knows, Mingus thought to herself.

She walked over to the television and sat down Indian-style in front of it. She felt like she was in grade school. Her spine curved over her lap. She was small. Small and being punished for something she had nothing to do with. She pressed power and play and watched something that couldn't have been real. It occurred to her to laugh. Laugh it all away and wake up again into a life she wanted. Where the people she loved were doing what they were supposed to do. She wanted a world where she could depend on them again. Where she could go back to being a successful lawyer about to get married with a semiperfect family. She could shine in that world. She would be happy there.

Carl played with Sarah and Ty. Brightly colored building blocks peppered the floor. There were books there. *Br'er Rabbit, Green Eggs & Ham, The Little Engine That Could.* He used to read those to her when she was little. She watched the way he held Sarah's face with both of his hands and kissed her forehead. How Sarah giggled so hard. Mingus wanted him to hold her face like that. Kiss her like that. She wanted to lay her head across his lap and cry. Tell him about every hurt that was wounding her heart. Tell him about Eric and Eva. Six months ago she would have run to him. Told him every small detail. But now, if she were to run to anyone, it would be M'Dea. M'Dea had been there.

When M'Dea arrived, Mingus had already watched the tape five times. She lay sideways on the couch with her coat balled up under her head, feet tucked just under her butt. She was to the part again where Glenda gave Sarah a bath.

M'Dea took off her coat and folded her dry cleaning over the arm of the couch. She sat down and pulled Mingus into her chest. Her chest was so warm. Mingus never remembered it feeling like that. Soft and safe. Mingus closed her eyes and burrowed closer to her mother's heartbeat as M'Dea stroked Mingus's hair with ring-less fingers.

Chapter 48

Sometimes you gotta sit back and take a hard long look at your life. Especially when sin done settled on your tongue and left a trail of bad-tasting witnesses. I ain't saying what I did was right. I am saying most days I don't see a better way of having done it. Hurtin' the people closest to me. Ellie, Glenda. Ain't nothin' nice about that. But hurtin' Mingus. Somethin' burns in the center of my chest every time I think about it. Like layin' on your back with 3:00 A.M. indigestion, but that ain't it. Only thing worse than hurtin' your child is not knowing how to explain why you did it. Ain't no answers for that. Even when I get down to the gritty of it. Knowin' I was greedy and tryin' to have everything all at once. Don't nothin' give justice to my baby's teardrops. The whys falling from her lips. The how-could-yous.

I was afraid. That's all I muster to say. Afraid and hopin' that somehow time would straighten out all the tangled ends I had thrown together. For me, the best part of being a man was being my girl's hero. Better than anything else in the world. It was too late for Eva and me, and I knew it, but Mingus, she always let me shine. I shined bright and big in her eyes. Bigger than I could ever hope to be anywhere else. And that's where the heartbreak comes in.

I fell. Not just because of the Ellie situation, Mingus coulda withstood that. But more so because of Sarah. Every time I think about the silence sittin' between us on the phone line, my heart tells me I shoulda said something sooner. I shoulda broke down and laid all my cards on the table. But it's one thing to fall from grace, it's something completely different when you step down. How was I supposed to step down from being the sun? I couldn't do it. Not after losing what I had spent the last thirty-five years of my life building. Everything was too much to risk losing. Not telling Mingus was my attempt to hang on to one of the most important parts of my life. And I won't apologize for that.

And when I'm all alone, no children, no Glenda. When I can forget the sound of my daughter's teardrops and how salt tracks musta ran the length of her face for days, I know I woulda lived this the same way a second time around.

I can't keep Mingus attached to my hip bone forever, I done tried that all her life. Wantin' to shield her from the nasty in this world. To look pretty in her eyes. People fall, they always fall. The more you tend to depending on yourself, the less you fall with 'em. Mingus needs to learn that, but that ain't something you can tell somebody outright. They got to figure it out in their own time. It's easier to stay down and not come back up again. That's what I coulda done stayin' with Ellie. Don't nobody have to agree with me. It may look ugly, but it's my ugly. That's what matters to me. I came back up again.

Chapter 49

December 28

I had imagined Christmas at my place.
M'Dea and Daddy coming by in the early afternoon
and staying into the evening. Eva showing up,
saying she had some party she had to go to,
that she could only stay a few minutes
and she'd end up staying three hours.
And though I had given up pork except for the occasional
pepperoni pizza or barbecued rib, I had imagined myself
baking a honey and pineapple ham with homemade macaroni
  and cheese
and fresh green beans with pearl onions.
M'Dea would have brought the cakes,
Eva the booze—it's kind of ironic now that I think about it.
And like always, Daddy would end up taking a nap
on the sofa after his second full plate and before his
  third.
He hasn't seen an entire football game

on Christmas in the last ten years.

Maybe he took a nap at Glenda's this year.

He didn't invite me. I didn't expect an invitation, I
wouldn't have gone anyway.

Even if we wouldn't have gotten into it. I never would have
thought I'd call my father out of his name. But that's what
he was to me at that moment.

A Punk Ass Nigga.

The words were like a plug in my throat. I couldn't
breathe unless I said it.

All he said back was I'm sorry you feel that way.

He wouldn't even argue with me.

He called to wish me a Merry Christmas anyway.

I wonder if he knows I got a Christmas card with a picture
of his new family on it. The handwriting wasn't his.

He was standing against a Christmas tree backdrop with a
red-and-navy tie

around his neck. Tyson's head hit just above his stomach.

Glenda, her hair long and blond again, sat with the baby on
her lap.

Her hands were so tiny. The length of half my index
finger.

There's still a part of me that wants to have a sister.

I wonder if maybe we'll be close someday.

M'Dea called early in the morning.

Said she was doing okay and that she'd be going to
North Carolina for a few days and not to worry about her.

She didn't say why she was going. I guess everybody
needs to get away sometimes.

I didn't hear from Eva. First time ever we didn't
at least call each other on a holiday.

I opened the gift she left at my door. Part of me thinks
that if it would solve

something I could hurt her back. And then I think, after
everything she did,

what else is there for her to lose. I don't really feel pain
about it anymore.

Just a numbness. A faint aching in my gut.

And then there's the part of me that's glad it happened.

I've had so many questions in my life about our
relationship,

since I was a little girl. At least now I know the questions
were answered

a long time ago. I just never paid attention.

I still slip and say his name sometimes.

Reach for him in my sleep. I actually started sleeping
with a pillow between my legs. That's the hard part of
letting go.

Trying to erase someone from your dreams.

I can't stop myself from wondering

why some people work out and we didn't.

Last night I thought I heard keys in the door. I wasn't
scared,

I just lay there and hoped it was him. The noise turned to
silence and thickened in

my ear. Maybe it was my imagination.

Maybe it was just me hoping.

I lay there wide awake, knowing I would have let him back
into my bed. Gladly.

I wouldn't have asked any questions. I wouldn't have
brought up the past.

We would have just been. No context. No pretext.

Just two people who loved each other suspended outside of
reality.

Outside of my feelings. I wouldn't have remembered how much he hurt me or how I'd lost everything in a matter of seconds. And as much as I'd always wanted my sister in my life, I know now I would have given her up in a heartbeat just to keep him. Not even forever, just for a little while.

Just for that night. I would give up everything valuable to me

just for him to hold me. For him to kiss me on the forehead and tell me

everything is going to be all right.

That's what makes me know the emptiness I feel is bigger than Eric.

How do you trust someone else more than you trust yourself?

I didn't cry when I took off the ring.

I just slipped it off. There was no imprint, no tan mark.

Just brown. Almost like it never happened. But it did happen.

I felt safe.

Like finally in my life I was doing something for me.

Something that had nothing to do with anyone else.

I should have taken off the ring sooner.

It's like I thought I was going to stop breathing when I did it.

I took it off anyway. I can only die so many times in this life.

And maybe death's not what I've been afraid of.

Chapter 50

I guess I felt it was time. I had been sittin' with them papers for a long while. Kept them in my saxophone case. Something about seeing the papers and the saxophone together made sense to me. Made me know I remembered how to give up something when I knew I had to. I gave Ellie the papers and she thanked me, dry-eyed. All the while I was crying on the inside. Looking for that last bit of love in her eyes I could hang on to. There wasn't anything left for me. All her love had been transferred somewhere else. As hard as I looked, I couldn't find it anywhere.

Chapter 51

It wasn't impossible to forgive him. It was hard, like returning the Snickers bar you stole when you were five or walking home on a sprained ankle. Mingus tallied the unfairness of the situation over and over again; heads she'd take him back, tails she wouldn't. Reality was she couldn't take him back, no matter how much she wanted to or how hard she tried. There was a block between them. The kind of thing that keeps hurt circulating long after the sin has passed. She refused to be bitter, though; bitterness is what drove Eva to do what she did. Mingus would keep her heart soft. She would be honest with herself about the difficulty of having a dream die while she watched it happen.

In a strange sort of way, Mingus was surprised it had taken Eva so long to score a major hurt. She had been trying for years, and Mingus had taken the fallout for the slightest possibility of having Eva in her life. With all the misgivings between them, it shocked Mingus that she hadn't seen something coming. Something had always been coming, but Mingus had wished for a sister for so long, it never occurred to her that Eva was it. Not the kind she wanted, but the kind she had—the kind that would hurt you most, because she was hurting.

Mingus sat in Eric's driveway with the motor running and the heater going full blast. On his latest nights, she knew he usually returned from work by eight. She sat behind the steering wheel, seat upright, consciously not listening to the radio. Every song— happy, sad, or otherwise—reminded her of Eric.

She hadn't spoken to him in three weeks, even though he'd left messages. For the first two days, she erased each message without listening to it. By day four, she had his pauses and breath patterns memorized. She reminded herself of her mother. The mother she'd grown up with, who had avoided making hard decisions in her life. Mingus didn't want to turn out that way. She didn't want to be married to someone she loved more than she loved herself. Look where that had gotten M'Dea.

It wasn't long before Eric's headlights flashed past her car and stopped short of the garage. He never dresses warm enough, Mingus thought. He walked toward her with both hands in his pockets wearing a black crewneck sweatshirt. Mingus rolled down the window.

"Hey," he said, looking as if he wanted to smile but was afraid to.

"Hey yourself," Mingus replied. "You have a few minutes?"

"Yeah."

"You can sit in the car if you like; it's a lot warmer."

Eric shrugged his shoulders and walked around to the passenger side. Mingus leaned over to unlock the door.

"You look nice."

"So do you," he said, getting into the car.

"I don't want to take up a lot of your time. I just, uh, I have some things that belong to you and I want to give them back."

"I don't want to hear this, Mingus."

She sucked her teeth. "I know. I don't want to do this either, Eric, but I have to."

"No you don't, not if you don't want to, Mingus—you don't."

He grabbed her hand. It felt so good to her to touch him again. She squeezed.

"I do have to. That's why I'm here."

He slipped his hand from hers.

"Well, I don't want it back, Mingus."

Tears started to crowd her eyes. The air shooting from the heating vent angled toward her face caused them to fall.

"Let's not make this ugly, okay?" He shook his head at her.

Mingus's voice raised an octave. "You can't imagine how hard this is. I don't want to do this; I need to."

"What about me, Mingus; I just proposed to—"

She grabbed his hand.

"I have to make this decision for me. I love you, but this isn't about you."

"You're giving me back my ring. How isn't it about me?"

"I need time. I need to do some things for myself."

"Do what?" He squeezed her hand gently. "What can't you do with me in your life?"

Mingus swallowed hard. Her words stuck like hard candy in her throat.

"Love myself. I've never done that. I've always relied on someone else to do it, even if they did it badly. I'd rather be with you than be with me and something's wrong with that." Mingus looked him in the eye and paused for a moment. "I'm afraid to be alone, Eric. I don't even like sleeping in a bed by myself—it shouldn't be this way."

Eric shook his head as she spoke. Mingus took her hand from his and reached behind the passenger seat. She grabbed a small box that held the engagement ring and both sets of his house keys.

"Here, Eric," she said, handing him the box. "I don't expect you to understand. I don't understand. I just know I have to make things right with myself."

He sat the box in his lap and held her hand tightly. His eyes were glassy, just like Eva's the first time Mingus ever saw her cry.

"So it's over?"

"For now, yes," her voice was barely a whisper.

Tears dropped from his eyes onto his jeans. "Not forever, right?"

Mingus didn't answer. Just held his hand as tightly as he held hers and hoped.

Acknowledgments

First I want to thank God Almighty for loving and blessing me in every situation. My mother, Bertha Dejan, for birthing me and giving me her honest eyes. My father, Virgil Adams, for being my backbone and, as I say in a poem written for him, *my first friend and best magic.* My sister, Jolena Jordan, for being the best sister and friend anyone could ask for. My older siblings, Lossie (whom I wanted to be just like growing up), Lydia, Robert, Morris, Virgil, and Fred. My nephew Rashaun for loving his Auntie Nonie. My uncle Dogan for always encouraging me. Monsha, Nickie, Michael, and all the rest of my family and loved ones who have supported and encouraged me along the way. My friend Nicole Valentine for being with me in the hard times and for all the tears and laughter we have shared. Edgar Brown, Kofi Bass and Richard May who have become more like big brothers than best friends (Kofi, yes, I said *big*). Nancy Padron, my second mama-sistah-girlfriend-voice-of-reason. Jaha Xanibu, Cherise Alley, and Xiomara Gumbs for all the healing conversations. Sherri White for her friendship and meditations. Natasha Gordon for hooking a sister up. Lawrence Hinkle, Esq. and JoAnn and Raymond Gallucio for being there. Wil Power, Derek McKeith, Eric Williams, Zi Malonga, and Ken and Lezlie Fence for their positivity. Gladys Steen and Alex Datcher for being two of the most beautiful women in my life. Jan Ebbey, Mr. Serrao, and Ms. Row for being my early teachers. Lady Walquer, master dancer and teacher, who has helped me to appreciate breath. Essie Ruffin for being a ninety-two-year-old wonder. Jewel Parker Rhodes, Mona Simpson, and Michael Levin for reading my work and giving honest criticism that helped me to grow. Sarah Jacobus, Sally, Noël, Ellery, Cynthia, and Asha for living their dreams with me. PEN Center USA West and UCLA Ext. Writing Program for the priceless opportunities. Wanda Coleman for being a safe harbor. Eugene Redmond for being a national treasure. Billy Higgins and Kamau Daaood for having a place like the World Stage exist. The World Stage poets and the Bush Women Writers for sharpening me. Iyara Fumilayo for being a catalyst for change in my life (you know the story—thank you). Tomika Washington of Lula Washington Dance Company for extending her art to me. Thank you to Malah, Jose Villamil, Leah Coley, Michelle Bee, and members of the LAPD for answering my questions and letting me into their stories. Tracy Sherrod, thank you for being beautifully you and giving me insight into my work. Jim Levine, thank you for being a wonderful agent and person—for all the times I've said thank you, there are a thousand more times I should have. I appreciate you greatly. My editor, Dominick Anfuso, you are a godsend, I can't say it any better than that. Thank you for believing in me; I'm glad to know you. Kristen McGuiness, thank you for keeping me calm. And lastly, thank you Michael Datcher for being my soulmate, confidant, colleague, prayer partner, and friend. You are brilliant and you above everyone have taught me how to live. Selah.